Staying Living and Lively,
in This Year

活著，在 這一年

林煥彰中英對照詩集

林煥彰著・黃敏裕譯
Poems by LIN, Fuan-chan
Translated by Min-Yu Morris HUANG

作者簡介

林煥彰，1939年生，台灣宜蘭人。二十歲開始學習寫作和畫畫，從事新詩、兒童文學創作與推廣。已出版相關著作110餘種，作品譯成多種外文發表及出版，並收入新加坡、台灣、香港、澳門、中國等中小學課文和教材，以及大學、中學學測考題和近百種選集。曾獲中山文藝獎，洪建全、陳伯吹、冰心、宋慶齡等兒童文學獎及澳洲建國二百周年現代詩獎章等。曾任聯合報系北美《世界日報》和泰國、印尼《世界日報》副刊主編；中華民國兒童文學學會、海峽兩岸兒童文學研究會理事長及亞洲兒童文學學會台北分會會長等。2008年春，應邀擔任香港大學首任駐校作家等。

LIN, Fuan-chan, born in 1939 in Yi-lan, Taiwan. Started learning to write and paint at 20 with focus on new poem writing, creative writing and promotion of children's literature and book writings; to date, with various publications of more than 110 book titles in different languages, some of which are used for teaching/learning materials or adapted into the primary and middle school textbooks in Singapore, Taiwan, Hong Kong and Macau, including test questions and many other hundreds of selections. Winner of the Chung Shan (Dr. Sun Yat-sen) Literature & Art Award; HONG Chien-chuan, CHEN Bo-chui, Bing-xin, SONG Mei-ling Children Literary Award and Medal Citation of the Bicentennial Celebration of the Founding of Australia and so on; Worked as Editor-in-Chief, Supplementary edition, "*United Daily News*" Group's North-America "*World News*;" editor in Thailand, Indonesia; President of the Society of the ROC Children's Literature; Association of the Across-the-Strait Children Literature Studies; and Taipei Chapter of the Asian Society of Children's Literature; In 2008, invited to be the first-term Residence Writer at Hong Kong University.

譯者簡介

黃敏裕，新竹高中／台灣師大英語系畢、臺北大學企業管理碩士；臺灣科技大學語言中心兼任講師、台灣專業英語文學會監事；English Career職場英文論壇總編輯、全球化教育推廣協會秘書長、美國教育測驗服務社ETS台灣區代表處學術顧問、Rotary Int'l District 3521基河網路扶輪社糾察RYLA主委；歷任美國新聞與世界報導中文周刊資深編譯、美國英語教師協會TESOL專業英文小組、美國文化及貿易中心資深專員、台北基督教青年會YMCA及財務經理學校英語講師。專長：職能英文基礎寫作ESP（English for Specific Purposes）；證照通過：觀光局觀光導遊人員、教育部國小英語師資。英文編譯：台北孔廟交趾陶藝術之美、陳牧雨書畫七十回顧展、韋啓義油畫收藏展，台北市文化局古蹟巡禮等。

Min-Yu Morris Huang/ Graduated from English Edu/Taiwan Normal University; MBA/Taipei University; Business Consultancy/Chung Hsing University; Licensed Tourist Guide/Tourism Bureau/Min. of Transportation; Certified Elementary English Teacher / Min. of Education; Worked part-time at NTUST Language Center, teaching basic English writing & career English; Editor, English Career /Global Education Association in Taiwan; Supervisor/Taiwan English for Specific Purposes/ESP Association; High School & YMCA Instructor; Senior Editor, Chinese Weekly *U.S, News & World Report, UDN*; Senior Cultural Affairs/Trade Promotion Specialist, Taipei American Cultural Center; Assistant Professor-level Expert, NTUST Continuing Education & Teaching Resource Center; Member/Director; RYLA, e-Hurricane Club/Rotary Int'l District 3521; TESOL USA; Publications: (translated into English) *CHEN Mu-yu, 70th Anniversary Retrospective Exhibit; WEI Chi-yi Oil Paintings Collections 2016; Taipei Confucius Temple Koji Pottery Art; Taipei Scenic sites/Historical Reservations (I & II)*

【作者序】
活著，在這一年

林煥彰

活著，在這一年，我做了什麼？

活著，什麼才叫活著？我喜歡問我自己；活著，活著的意義是什麼？

活著，不是只有呼吸、吃飯而已；總該做點什麼？我做了什麼？

寫詩，是我一輩子的志趣；所謂志趣，我認為是自始至終、一輩子都不會改變的興趣，所以寫詩，我會一直寫，一直寫……

「活著，認真寫詩；死了，讓詩活著。」我就秉持這份詩觀，追求我要寫的詩。

這一年，我指的是2017年，是我寫詩最豐收的一年；總計大約有250首以上。

我寫的詩，包括一個字或三五行的小詩，長的有多達三四十行以上；寫詩，我有為兒童寫的，叫兒童詩，有為我自己寫的，稱為成人詩；其實，在我心目中，不論我寫的兒童詩，或成人詩，都是為我自己，但也可以和別人分享，因為我愛使用淺白文字書寫，希望讀者樂於親近，同時我也會投稿、發表，出版、發行。

近年我的足跡走過很多地方，從我的住家汐止研究苑社區出發，我去過了中國大陸的北京、南京、成都、漳州、福州、廈門、海滄、武漢、武夷山、青島、嶗山……，泰國的曼谷、清邁、清萊、巴達雅……，澳洲的坎培拉、黃金海岸、墨爾本、雪梨……，南韓的首爾、慶州、全州、釜山，以及台灣的離島──金門、馬祖等，所以我養成了隨時隨地、可以在路上寫詩；包括在社巴、公車、捷運、地鐵、高鐵、飛機……，所以我寫我的生活，也寫我的心，也拿詩當日記：每寫一首，我都會註記寫作日期、時間和地點；當然，也包括我的所思所想所見所聞，等等。

今年，2018年，我按計畫，在五月已出版了一本生肖畫的詩畫集《犬犬・謙謙・有禮》（台北・秀威），給成人看的；另一本《我的貓是自由的》，大約十月中會在湖南長沙出版，是給兒童看的；還有兩本，原來都不在計畫之內，一本《詩，花或其他》，已獲宜蘭縣政府文化局補助，列入「蘭陽文學叢書」，預計11月出版，一本《截句，不純為截句》，四行以內小詩，111首，應邀列入台灣詩學社叢書，12月自費出版；而這一本《活著，在這一年》，本來也不在計畫之內，需要自己花錢，但也因為有了英文翻譯的緣故，同時藉以作為自己紀念年屆八十、寫詩六十周年，於是設法一起推出。

當然，有關這些詩的寫作和出版，由於自己平時的勉力，也因為有很多貴人支持、鼓勵和協助，是我所必須藉此表達由衷感激和不能或忘的恩澤。以這本《活著，在這一年》中英對照詩集的順利出版，如果沒有貴人黃敏裕教授一整年的義務翻譯，如果沒有女詩人郭至卿的引介，我是永遠也不會有這份榮幸的。

　　我的詩的外文翻譯，過去雖也有些出版，包括英、日、韓、泰、德、俄、蒙等十餘種外文，除了韓文版《林煥彰詩選》（首爾・漢聲）、中英泰文和中英韓文版《孤獨的時刻》（台北・蘭亭／首爾・漢聲）外，大都還是屬於零星的在報刊、選集中發表，能有《活著，在這一年》的出版，我是極為感謝黃敏裕教授。有了英文的譯本，我想一定會有更多機會、以詩這份善良的語言和我真誠的心意，與世界各國擁有共同理念的同好分享和交流，這是我最感欣慰和感激的。

2018.08.16 八十生日前夕・研究苑

【 Foreword 】
Being Alive, Fully Living with Poetry the Whole Year

LIN, Fuan-chan／
Authored by LIN Huan-chang

Being alive living, in the year of 2017, what have I been doing?

Living, what's meant by living? I like to ask myself: "Living, what's the meaning of being alive and fully living?

Living, it's not just breathing, eating; there's something more to do? What have I been doing then?

Writing poems, it's my lifelong passion and aspiration, which is, from start to finish, my unchanging interest the whole life; therefore, I will keep on writing poems, on and on, without stopping....

"Being alive, living earnestly with poem writing; until the heart stops beating, let the poems last and keep living on." Firmly upholding and sticking to this passage to the world of poetry, seeking for writing my desired poems.

In the good-harvest bump year of 2017, a most fruitful year for poetry-writing, in totality, there are approximately more than 250 poems completed.

The poems I wrote include those little or mini poems with only one single Chinese character or word, and three- or five-liners, as well as the longer ones comprising thirty or even forty lines; I compose poems - some for children called children's poems, some written for myself, called adult or grown-up poems; in my mind, no matter what readers they are written for, children or grown-ups, they are actually composed for myself which may also be shared with others because I love to use the simple, easy and plain language to compose poems, hoping to have readers like to get close to such verses or poems; at the same time, I will contribute, issue, release, publish and distribute them to the public.

In recent years, I have travelled at lot, been to many places leaving my footprints; setting out from my community residence studio in Xi Zh, I have been to many cities or towns in Mainland China including Beijing, Nanjing, Cheng-du, Zhang-zhou, Fu-zhou, Xia-men, Hai-chang, Wu-han, Wu-Yi Shan, Qing-dao, Lao Shan and so on; in Thailand, been to Bangkok, Chiang-mai, Chiang-rai, Bataya...; in Australia, been to Canberra, Brisbane Golden Coast, Melbourne, Sydney; in South Korea, been to Seoul, Gyeong-ju, Jeom-ju and Bu-san as well as Taiwan's off-shore islets - King-men and Ma-tsu and so on.

Such frequent traveling and moving activities, therefore, trained me to develop a habit of writing poems whenever and wherever I am, be it on the road along the way to and from the destinations; for example, in the community shuttle buses, public buses, Mass Transport/MRT cars, subways, high speed railways, airplanes..... Certainly they all comprise what I think, ponder, see and hear, experience...and so on.

This year, in 2018, I published on schedule, in May a themed collection of 12 animal symbolic signs to denote human birth year, namely *Pictures and Poems on Dogs and Puppies*, entitled ***Qian Qian Punned Doggies as Humble Modest and Polite as a Gentleman*** (Hsiu Wei, Taipei) designed for adult or grown-up readers; another one entitled, ***My Kitten that's Free*** that's about to be published in Chang-sha, China, in October, designed for children.

There are two more book projects originally not in my planned schedule: one is, ***Poetry, Flowers and Others*** which is already funded by the Bureau of Culture of the Yi-lan County Government as listed in the ***Lan Yang Literature Book Series*** scheduled for the publication in November, a collection entitled, ***Truncated Sentences, Not Purely for Cut-off Verses and Sentences***," with mini poems consisting of less than four lines with some 150 pages, has been invited to be listed in the ***Taiwan Poetry Society Series***, a self-funded book project to be printed out in December. As regards this one ***Being alive fully Living with Poetry the Whole Year*** also self-funded though not in my original planned schedule, yet being my first project with English translation version side by side going with the original work, to make its debut simultaneously in the celebration of my 80th birth year as well as the 60th anniversary of my career for poem writing.

Certainly, regarding the writing and publishing of these poems, it is not just attributable to my everyday striving efforts in the pursuit of my interest, but also to so many right helpers or benefactors coming to me at the right time, for whom I have to hereby express my hearty gratitude for their unselfish support and unexpected kindness. The most recent example is the successful publication of this bilingual collection of my poems, ***Being Alive Fully Living with Poetry the Whole Year*** by the volunteer translator Mr. Morris Min-yu HUANG for his earnest efforts expended the whole year efforts in striving to read and put them into English, through the introduction of Poet Writer Ms. GUO, Zhi-qing with whom I took the pleasure and honor to make the acquaintance several years ago.

Over the past years, my poems, though occasionally being translated into and published in more than 10 foreign languages including the English, Japanese, Korea, Thai, German, Russian and Mongolian versions, where, besides the Korean edition: ***Selected Poems by LIN Fan-chang*** (Seoul, *Han Voices*), and editions of Chinese English and Thai, and Chinese English and Korean, ***The Lonely Moments*** (Lan-ting, Taipei/*Han Voices*, Seoul), others we sporadically or occasionally published or released in some journals or collections of poems. I am most grateful to Mr. HUANG Min-yu whose significant contribution and consistent efforts help make possible the publication of this ***Being alive Fully Living with Poetry the Whole Year***. With this English version going out, I believe there will be ever more opportunities for us all, to use the good, true language of poetry combined with my truest and sincerest thoughts from the bottom of my heart, to reach out, to interact with the international like-minded friends of poetry for the sharing and exchange of common beliefs, views, ideas and thoughts.

At Studio Residence, 8/16/2018 on Birthday Eve

【譯者序】
寫在林煥彰中英對照詩集《活著，在這一年》之前

黃敏裕

除了深入淺出底哲思與輕快純真底童心，
我們還能從他的人生漫談慧語學到什麼？
這冊花開並蒂，中英並茂詩集
從中英詩文的賞讀習作，一舉兩得

既提升流暢中文表達力，也打開國際英語習用的一盞燈、一扇窗
更將帶給您對目下生活、周遭環境及人生當下、意味來由及終極目的
觸發積極、深刻的省思與當即著手實踐，開創一個迥然不同底人生

　　今年三月，一向謙卑自牧，終身自強不息的煥彰老師親駕我任教的台灣科技大學，
拎著兩冊他的詩畫集：《犬犬‧謙謙‧有禮》、《先雞‧漫啼‧大吉》，暢談他的年度
新書出版構思與規畫，看他已是髦耋之年，仍眉飛色舞，神采奕奕，每天為他的明天、
下個月、新的年度，籌謀些什麼，規劃出什麼，不為稻糧謀也無補於國計民生，只是風
塵僕僕，奔走出席於各種活動，推動熱切生活即能靈動的活性文學，提升優雅文化以美
化人生，其精神與精力之旺盛，讓人打心底感動、景仰與效法；譬如，他自2015年起進
行每年出版十二生肖畫詩畫集，這回來訪，我本以為輪到豬了，想不到是這一年的隨時
隨地勤耕、牧雲的結集，而且隨著這些年來，雲遊四海，擴展胸懷，把目標訂在雙語國
際化，期能讓垂髫幼童，打開視野，及早中英並茂，同步演習；為人爸媽，鶴髮老者，
也能秉持老師一般的人生信念，終身學習，活到老學到老。
　　綜觀全書，雖不見我那定居於澳洲雪梨女兒生肖的豬影，卻有一隻擬人化，跳脫
個人說理，融入老師自個兒心路、生活、思慮及七情八慾，喜怒哀樂的貓，大行其道，
娓娓貓理；這倒使我想起月前才在花博公園參觀卡通動畫變裝博覽會，看到由美國最夯
Steven Universe所文化創意般的產物Peridot Kitten一個小屁貓與Steven的貓畫貓化一起日
常生活的故事，也透過YouTube影視頻，吸引了全球無數青少年，甚至成年人的青睞，
莫非身為「貓心理學家」的煥彰師，也貼近並趕上時潮脈搏，抓得住我們青年人的心？
返老還童，以孩子為師？然而，從十二生肖外一章的貓主題切入，他始終也是一以貫
之，是以「童趣盎然、生活哲思及無盡愛心」（見宋熹，序〈詩散文的哲思，或者生活
的散文詩－－林煥彰詩畫集《犬犬‧謙謙‧有禮》〉來記錄這一年來，國內外之所聞所
見所感所思所淬鍊出的人生輕鬆漫談與智慧雋語，分享詩人之國的大小人讀者，甚至可
藉由這冊中英雙語詩集，也惠及海外學中文的兒童與研習華語的大眾呢！

　　個人從服務二十六年的美國文化中心提前退休以來，轉換跑道，愛上教書，更愛上推動兒童語文教育，以提升其口語寫作表達之流暢，尤其在2000年接受過「國小英語教師甄試培訓」後的我，深深體會中英口語寫作，透過簡易明白、流暢有趣的詩歌韻文文字，將可有效同時提升雙語的互通與發展。

　　之後，在退休這十年來，除了兼課與在家照顧重病家人外，就是全心全力幫助英文編譯工作，包括：《台北市文史古蹟手冊》、《龐曾瀛畫冊》、《韋啟義油畫收藏畫展》、《陳牧雨七十回顧展》等；尤其馬英九市長序台北市孔廟編印《孔廟交趾陶之美》中英對照版，在諸多壁畫圖版中，就屬「孔子問禮老子」與「孔子師項橐」兩幅最讓人印象深刻。

　　這也是我對煥彰師最欽佩之處之一。打從跟小孩一塊讀《國語日報》，林良專欄兒歌、童詩、散文起，奠定了語文基石，如今頗思把美好的中文也變成簡易曉暢的英文，將詩人植基於中華傳統文化觀念之心思、想法或看法「外銷」出去，一如當年國內翻譯那麼多西洋兒童文學詩歌名著，滋養成長了我們的心智與心靈一般，因此，我樂於為詩人煥彰師這一年的新作，一一譯成英文，我們也因此順利的共同擁有了一本雙語書。

【 Foreword for English Translation 】
Being Alive, Fully Living with Poetry the Whole Year

Authored by LIN Fuan-chang

What else could we learn from this philosophic poet's thoughts and children-like light pure heart
This bilingual book like two flowers growing on the same base symbolizing good luck
Enjoy Chinese and English poems and learn to read and write, killing two birds with one stone!

This collection not only helps advance your skill in fluent Chinese expression, but also in using plain English to lighten up your learning of both languages through a global window to
Further open up a brand-new life by use and practice of the author's insights, views, reflections on the present moment of life, the world around us and what we are and where we're going

This year, last March, Teacher Fuan-chang, the always humble, modest and self-disciplined gentleman, a life-long learner constantly striving to self-improve, visited my office at the National Taiwan University of Science and Technology, with his two newly issued books on his drawings and poems, "***Humble Courteous Dogs, in a Refined and Civil Manner,***" and "***A Pioneer Chicken First Crowing Wide and Loud for Big Good Luck.***" We had a happy, upbeat energized conversation on his new year's publishing plans.

I've been deeply moved from the bottom of my heart, thus admiring and emulating him a lot for his constantly earnest and vigorous efforts expended on passionately promoting an enthusiastic life with poetry and literature for leading to build an elegant, beautiful lifestyle for all, by frequently joining the related programs and activities despite his old age in late seventies. He's working so hard absolutely not for his own gains and fame or large-scale national strategies, but quietly and conscientiously striving to reach his self-imposed lifelong goals and ideals on a daily basis to make his schedule for the next month, new year, or even tomorrow!

For example, since 2015, he launched his annual publishing schedule for his collections of poems and paintings based on a series of 12 Chinese zodiac animals one after another; this year at the call of his, I had assumed it would be a hog in the advent of 2019, the year of the pig. No. Surprisingly, he has a plan to debut a first-ever bilingual collection of his poem written diligently anytime and anywhere around this year, in Taiwan and abroad with more and more lecturing trips and shows overseas. He aimed such an endeavor to share his broad writing and learning experiences with more children to open their eyes and minds by starting as early as possible to be a bilingually spoken global citizen; at the same time, their parents even, grannies can also learn with and from their kids to live up to his life-long belief in "Live and Learn."

Throughout the book, though devoid of any pigs or hogs which are also the horoscope or zodiac symbol sign of my daughter who lives in Sydney, Australia; instead, there is a personified cat on behalf of Teacher Fuan Chang to chat on morals not preach to circumvent the conventionally teaching way by cherishing and integrating his own thoughts, life experiences and stories, joy, tempers, sadness and happiness as reflected by this free cat, the cute yet thoughtful and disciplined kitten. This reminds me of the Peridot Kitten of the USA characterized by Steven Universe I came across last month at the Exhibition of Animations and Cos-playing in the Floral Expo Themed Park whose everyday life via YouTube has been attracting the fans, young and old, around the world.

I'm wondering how the "Cat Psychologist" Teacher Fuan-chang could also have caught the fashionable train to be so trendy as to get close to the mind of the teenagers. Is he turning younger himself again like a kid, learning from the youngsters? Still, with such a theme focused on kitten going beyond the 12 zodiac animals, as usual, he sticks to his well-known characteristic features; namely, "being full of childhood fun and joy, rooted deep in his life philosophy and insights, with the endless love for humans and nature," as quoted from the preface by Song Xi – Poetic Prosaic and Philosophic Thoughts, Or Living Prosaic Poems" in the book entitled. "Qian Qian Humble and Modest, Being Refined and Polite." All the readers, young and old, can all benefit from his casual talks, light-hearted sayings, daily-life mottos, words of wits and wisdom as abstracted and condensed from what he has felt, heard, seen, and thought, home and abroad, around the year. Moreover, published in such a bilingual form, it can also benefit all the Mandarin Chinese learning public.

After an early retirement from my 26-year service for the American Trade/ Cultural Center in Taipei, I've chose my first love for teaching and writing, in particular, promoting children's language education with an aim at directing and advancing their fluent oral and writing communication from the start through reading and basic writing. Luckily, I got passed the 2000 Education Ministry's primary school English teachers certificate test and received the training, and that made me realize none the less the importance of teaching basic oral and writing through interesting, simple and plain, clear and fluent rhymed verses and essays, if likely via the use of concurrently developing and interchanging bilingually language teaching and learning.

After that, over the ten years, besides teaching and home-caring for family members, I have devoted much of my time and energies to helping with some English translation projects, including a *Bilingual Guide to Taipei City Cultural and Historical Sites ad Preservations,*

"*Collections of Paintings by PANG Tseng-ying, Painting Collection* by WEI Chi-yi, CHEN Mu-yu's 70th Year Anniversary Retrospective Exhibition." Noteworthy is the bilingual publication of "*Beauty of the Koji Pottery Art – Taipei Confucius Temple*" prefaced by former Mayor MA Ying-jeou, where I was most impressed with the two ceramic wall pictures depicting "Confucius Consulted Lao Dan or Lao-tzu on Rituals and Etiquette" and "Confucius Modestly and Humbly Learned from Xiang Tuo, an 8-year-old kid."

That is why and how much I have admired and respected Teacher Fuan-chang most. As early as reading the *Guo Yu Daily News* – for Mandarin Chinese language with my kids of such genres and forms of writing as kids' songs, poems and essays from the two well-known Teachers Fuan-chang and LIN Liang who helped greatly build our solid foundation for Chinese language reading and writing. Today I sincerely hope to make such beautiful Chinese into simple and plain, fluent and interesting writings to be made for its equivalent English learning and teaching materials that have based on traditional Chinese culture and philosophy, thus "exporting" what we feel, think, or see just as we "did import" so many translations of famous western poetry and literature books that have nourish and enrich our mind and intellect. I am therefore pleased to recommend Teacher Fuan-chang's new book for the year 2008 that is translated into English to make possible the smooth debut of such a bilingual book of his poetry.

目次

我的小雞的祕密

我的小雞，是我畫的，
各個都有牠們自己的
祕密的祕密；我的小雞
牠們是很好奇的，而且是
天生的，各個都很好奇。

我的小雞，牠們整天都很愛玩
各個都很忙，各個都
愛東跑西跑，有什麼發現
誰都不會告訴誰；

也不必告訴誰，自己就把它先吃掉
誰也不知道誰發現了什麼
什麼樣的祕密；別人不知道的
什麼是什麼，
這就是最保險的，祕密的祕密。

（2017.03.09／07:24 研究苑）

The Secret Kept by My Chicks

My chicks, all are my drawings,
Each of them has kept their own
Secret to all the secrets; my chicks,
They're curious, and
Born so, for all of them are very curious

My little chicks, all of them love playing all day long
Each of them is very busy, everyone loves to go here and there in all directions whenever they find
  anything
No one will tell anyone else;

Nor does anyone need to tell others; they prefer to eat it up first by themselves
No one knows who finds
What kind of secret; that others do not know,
what's what either,
That's the safest thing to do, keeping the secret of the secrets from others.

紫斑蝶的春天

春天未必都要屬於我，
春雨綿綿，屬於雲和雨
也屬於雲和霧
如有陽光，我需要陽光

紫斑蝶需要花，花和她
也都需要陽光；我們一起讚美
有陽光的春天，她屬於大地
我們也屬於她……

（2017.03.25／08:25 在回礁溪的首都客運上）

The Spring for Purple-spot Butterflies

Spring doesn't necessarily belong to me,
The Spring drizzle continuously falling persistently, which belongs to clouds and rains
Also it's a part of cloud and fog
If there's any sunshine, I will need the sunshine

Purple-spotted butterflies need flowers; both flowers and
They also need the sunshine; let's together praise the sunshine
The sunshining spring, that belongs
To the great earth
Which we also belong to ……

童年在等我

是童年走得太快了嗎？
我，十五歲才離開故鄉；
是我走得太慢了嗎？
為什麼要人家等我？

我，一年一年的年老了
步伐一定慢下來；童年還是
十五歲以前那個童年，活蹦亂跳
歲月，當然可以往前衝
怎會有上了年紀的人，能夠趕上？

不必等了！等了也白等，
老，必須就要承認
哪有人不老？童年，照說
他也應該老了，幾十年過去了？他的面貌，也會大大改變
即使他此刻現在站在我面前，
我也不認得了，那娃娃的臉兒
憨憨厚厚的直樸的模樣，是多麼的
令人羨慕呀！
如果我是他，我也該多雀躍！
好啦！他還算是不錯的

十分念舊，又相當有耐心；不過，
我還是會相當懷疑，他怎麼能認出我？

現在，我必須加快腳步，一直往前走
讓我趕上了他；當我看到他的時候，
我該怎麼開口向他打招呼，說出第一聲

嗨咿──，感謝您
還在等我！

（2017.03.28／21:08 在回山區的社巴）

Childhood, Is Waiting for Me over There!

Has the childhood been walking away from me way too fast?

Me, I didn't leave my hometown until I was fifteen;

Was I walking too slowly?

Why did I want others to wait for me?

Me, I'm getting older and older year by year

My walking pace must be slowing down; the childhood still

Remains to be that very one before I was 15 of age, when I was always so lively and actively skipping

  dancing and jumping about, full of energy and vigor

Over the years being passing, I may certainly be marching forward

How could people so aged like me catch up with them moving at such a fast speed?

No need to keep waiting! All the waiting is useless,

Getting old, one must admit it and face the fact.

How can it be possible that men could not get old? Naturally to say,

The look of that childhood, should also be drastically changed after several decades of years are gone?

Even if it were standing in front of me right now,

I couldn't even recognize it any more, I mean its baby-like face

How innocent and naive that look would look so adorable, likable and adorable and admirable!

If I were him, I'd be so happy as to jump, skip and leap here and there around like those happy birds and

  sparrows!

Alright! Still, he's not so bad

So very much nostalgic and homesick, and rather patient; however,

I'm rather suspicious, wondering how come he could still recognize me?

Now. I must quicken my steps, moving forward all the way straight ahead

Let me catch up with him; when I see him,

How could I open my mouth to greet him, uttering my first word

Hey You--thank you, sir

You're still waiting for me!

春天的早晨

這是春天的早晨，
有陽光的春天的早晨，
有鳥聲的，春天的早晨
媽媽要我洗自己的衣服；

有陽光，它讓我看到什麼地方
該好好洗，又搓又揉；
有鳥聲，鳥有五色鳥
鳥有八哥，鳥有白頭翁
鳥有綠繡眼、杜鵑和斑鳩，
牠們都是我家的好鄰居，
都住在我家門前的樹林裡；
有的在桂花樹上，有的在高高的
綠竹中，也有的在更高的茄苳樹上
牠們唱歌，牠們稱讚我
我很高興，也很有耐心的
把每件衣服都很用心
搓搓揉揉，洗得乾乾淨淨。

（2017.03.29 青年節／10:23 研究苑）

Spring Morning

This is a spring morning,

The spring morning basking in the sunshine,

The spring morning, with birds chirping and twittering

Mama wants me to do my own laundry.

There's the sunshine, that let me see clearly somewhere my clothes that

I should wash hard, with more scrubbing and more rubbing;

There are birds singing, including *Psilopogon nuchalis* or five-colored birds,

There are Mynah or Ba-ge, Chinese Bulbul or white-headed (Taiwanese: peʰ-thâu-khok-á)

There are Zosterops japonicus or Japanese White-eyes, cuckoos and turtle-doves,

They're all my good neighbors;

They're living in the forest in front of my house;

Some are perching on the sweet-scented osmanthus trees, while some are higher up

In the green bamboo trees; still more are on the much higher *Bischofia javanica egg plant winter trees*

They're singing; they're praising me

I'm very pleased and delighted, also very patient

In washing carefully and earnestly each and every piece of my clothes

Scrubbbing and rubbing them very hard, into great and perfect neatness and tidiness.

春天，賴床有理

春天是有賴床的理由；

不是她賴床，是我賴床
我已經讓綠繡眼、五色鳥、八哥
輪流叫過了我一個早上，

又將接近晌午，我還賴著
賴在昨夜沒有睡過的床上！

昨晚，那是她先邀我的
邀我為她寫詩，她
就是春天，還有另外一位

她，是主管寫詩的女神
叫繆斯！

不管怎麼說，反正是
昨晚沒有睡好，應該說

沒有睡，因為她們要我寫詩
一起寫詩，這是一項挺美好的事

平時寫詩，哪還有誰陪你？
尤其夜晚，該睡而不睡的時候

尤其是兩位都是美女，
春天和詩的女神；
是的。我應該要有一首好詩，送給她們，

我不能憑白讓人家徹夜陪我，
而一無是處，浪費那千載難逢的
春天的夜晚的一樁美事！
熬過了一夜，磨墨一樣

夜是越磨越黑，越黑越稠
包括睡眠，
一個字也沒能寫下，夜是那麼難熬
詩不是很容易就能被你逮到嗎？
不是的，她比泥鰍、鰻魚還要滑溜；

明明是可以說
我愛妳，我卻不能寫
我愛妳！這是有很大的差別，
差別就在於你不懂含蓄，

你不懂人家的心理；春天和繆斯
她們都不會這樣喜歡你，她們都不會那麼直白的讓你
直白下去！
這一夜就這一夜這樣要折磨你，
磨了一夜，一首小詩都還不知道
她在哪裡？

綠繡眼、五色鳥、八哥
還有更遠的藍鵲，牠們都很賣力
已經輪流叫過了你
好幾遍，你，你，你
你，還賴在昨晚一直沒有睡過的
那張床上！

（2017.03.30／13:53 研究苑）

Springtime Are Good for Hanging on and Staying in Bed

In springtime there are good reasons for us to linger in bed

It's not she who hangs on staying in bed; it's me who lingers in bed

I already let all the following chirping and twittering in the ears the entire morning; they include:
  Japanese White-eyes or Zosterops japonicus, *Psilopogon nuchalis* or five-colored birds, and, blank-browed, mynas or Ba-Ge or Mynah

So as they take turns to have waken me up the whole morning,

Again it's going to be near the noon, yet I'm still staying

Hanging on in my bed that I haven't slept on last night!

Last night, it's she who took the initiative to
invite me to write poems for her. She's
Spring; there's another
She who is the goddess in charge of poetry writing
Named Muses!

No matter what I say, thin or thick, I didn't have a sound sleep last night,

Or exactly I hadn't slept at all, because they wanted me to write poems
Writing poems together, that's a pretty beautiful thing to do

In a normal day writing poems, is there anyone else who would accompany you?
Especially in the night time, when it's time to go bed. Yet I didn't sleep

Especially when both of them are beauties,
The goddesses of spring and poetry,

Yes. I'd have written a good poem, to send to them as gifts.

I just can't let others freely accompany me throughout the entire night,
But I'm so insignificant a nobody, wasting that hard-to-get time in one thousand years

The night in Spring is a beautiful thing to cherish

Euduring the beautiful thing last night, I like rubbing the ink stick upon the ink slab stand.

Tortured through that dark night, is as black as the dark ink, like rubbing and milling black ink stick on the ink-stone,

In the night it is like ink stick on the stone slab; the harder and thicker one mills, the more darkened the night turns,

including sleeping,

Not a single word can be written, and the night is so hard to endure or tolerate

Isn't it so easy for you to catch the poems?

No, it isn't; it's more slippery than mud fish or loaches or eels;

Even it may be free and natural to say

I love you, yet I can't write it to express it so

I love you! There's a sharp difference between the two.

The difference lies in whether or not you understand what's meant by "reserved or implicit," in wording

You don't read the mind of others; springtime and Muses

They both don't like you in such a way, nor do they like you in such a straightforward and explicit way to let you

Continue to be so direct and explicit!

This night. It's this very night when you're subject to be so tortured,

Taking pains for the whole night's torturing, I couldn't even have any little poem written out.

Where's she?

Japanese White-eys, black browed barbets, mynas, Chinese bulbul, ba-ge

And further faraway Urocissa caerulea or the blue lark, all of which have strived really hard to

Have taken turns to wake you up

Crying and shouting many times, calling you, you, you

You, still you are hanging on lingering there where you hadn't slept at all night yesterday.

On that very bed!

通泉草的小祕密

通泉草，牠們知道哪裡有泉水
春天來就開著小花，有人說，她們開花朵朵都是
花蝴蝶；我說，
她們都擁有自己的祕密；
說是祕密，其實她們還是樂於公開
和大家分享；每一朵小花兒都是
一個可親可愛的小女孩的
臉蛋兒，每一個都笑得很開心──
其實，我正要說的還是
她們各個都擁有一個共同的祕密，
不必說你也可能已經發現到──
每一朵小花兒都是一個小娃兒，
她們開開心心的笑著的小臉蛋兒，
你知道的，她們各個都是俏皮的
吐著小小的舌尖兒，要告訴你
哪兒有清涼甘甜的泉水，──
這就是她們要公開的小祕密。

（2017.03.31／00:00 研究苑）

A Secret to the Spring-sourced Grass

Spring-sourced grass, knows where to link or access to a water source

When spring comes, it sprouts out small flowers in full bloom,

Some say, every flower gets blooming is

A flower butterfly; I say,

They all have got and kept their own secret;

Even if it's said to be a secret, in fact, they're glad and ready to publicize or release it.

To share with all; every small flower is

An affectionate, lovely face of a little cute girl;

All the lovely girls are smiling really happily and joyously——

In fact, what I'm going to say still is

Each of them has shared their own common secret,

Needless to say, you might have already found that——

Each and every small flower is a little cute baby,

Their happily and cheerfully smiling little faces

You know something, each of them is a cute and naughty girl

Poking out their small tongues, when they're sprouting out the budding, wanting to tell you

Where there's cool sweet spring water located——

That's the little secret they have wanted to publicize and announce to the world.

約會，我選擇春天

今天，我要去和常玉約會；
我選擇春天，春天有很多機會
春天有很多可能有機會，我可以看到很多
會走動的花，
她們都是常玉常畫的美女，
在巴黎的春天的街道
她們也有可能，都不穿衣服
就像春天的每朵花兒，
該開就開的花，賞心悅目
也有很多可能，我會有機會
看到常玉畫的每一位美女；
我可以很自在的，很自由的
選擇，近距離的
站在她們面前，慢慢欣賞
也有可能，一個人自己發呆
不知會想些什麼，
常玉也可能不曾想過的，
我就一一替他想了……

（2017.04.13／12:23 捷運小南門／去看常玉特展之前）

To Make a Date with Spring Chosen

Today, I want to have a date with Chang Yu;

I chose spring, which has got many opportunities

In spring there will be many possibilities, which I may be able to see

Many flowers that can walk,

They're beauties being frequently painted by Chang Yu,

In Paris on the streets spring is very much in the air

They' re all likely, not to wear clothes

They're all like every flower in spring,

Those flowers are in full bloom at the blooming dates, to please the heart and eyes

Also there are many possibilities for me,

To be able to see every beautiful girl Chang Yu painted,

Whom I can choose at ease, very freely

to get very close to them from a very short distance

Standing in front of them, too slowly and closely stare and gaze at them

Also very likely, me I can just be there alone stone-dumped

Not knowing what else to think about that even Chang Yu hasn't thought of it either,

What Chang Yu hasn't thought of.

I'll think it over for him one by one……

誤診

春天，什麼都有可能
有位精神科醫師診斷：
他的心不見了！

他，就是我
我是好好的，還想著一個人
但醫生還是堅持：
他的心，被偷走了

夜夜有夢！

（2017.04.15／08:52 捷運永安市場）

Mis-diagnosis

In spring, everything is possible to happen
In a report on a mental disease diagnosed with by the doctor:
His heart is out of sight!

That He, that is me
Me, I'm all right, but still I'm thinking about someone else
But the doctor still insists:
His heart, is stolen

Every night, he dreams sweet dreams!

我想，想想

莫非我是什麼都沒有，又比什麼都有的
還富有，要不我怎麼能夠
在幾個有限的文字裡，找到了我的
孤獨純真的心，我的早已不再去想它的
過去的悲與喜

莫非人家什麼都有的，比起我的
什麼都沒有的孤寂窮困，連一顆小小的
心，也都保不住的這些那些？

莫非真的是什麼都是莫非的什麼都不是的，又什麼都是
想想，什麼都有的和什麼都沒有的
我，常常想什麼都該有什麼都該沒有
也是一種有。

（2017.04.30／06:59 研究苑）

I'm Thinking, and Pondering or Reflecting

Doesn't that mean I don't have anything, yet I have more than anything else,

Thus wealthier than anyone else; otherwise, how could it be

Possible for me

To discover to find from among the limited words, found

My lonely pure and true heart, that I've no longer thought of those things sad and joyous in the past

Doesn't it mean that other people have everything, better than what I've had now

with nothing but my loneliness and poverty; worse, not even my little tiny heart

That can't hold these and those things in check or in store there?

Doesn't it mean that indeed what it is the same as what is not

Just pondering on everything you've had and everything you've not had

Me, I'm always reflecting what I should've had, and what I shouldn't have had

It's too a kind of what I've had in some sense.

五峰旗和二龍村

一山一水，有山有水
我的故鄉，在礁溪；
是祖先流浪的終點，
是我流浪的起點……

山，雪山一重又一重
綿延千萬重，重重壓著
離鄉背井的人，
越去越遠……

水，二龍一程又一程
蜿蜒千萬里，小河大河
流向大海
我也不復返

五峰旗，一座瀑布
一疊又一疊，摺成五層
層層書寫，流逝的塊疊

二龍村，二龍一河
上接汨羅江，年年端午可聽到
屈原離騷，千年悲歌
鑼鼓喧天，詩祭千年……

（2017.05.14 母親節／07:42 研究苑）

Wu Feng Qi and Er-long Village

One mountain one water; there are mountains and waters
My hometown, in Chiao-his(Jiao-xi);
It's the destination of my ancestors' wandering journey,
It's the starting-point of my wandering ......

Mountains, Snow mountains ranges, one layer on another
Extending and lingering a thousand and ten thousand layers, one pressing another
Those going away from home,
Leaving the nativetown farther and farther......

Waters, Er-long one journey after another
Meandering a thousand and ten thousand kilometers, small rivers and large rivers
Flowing into the huge sea, with no return
Me, I'm not returning, too

Wu Feng Qi, a water fall
One layer on another, being folded into five layers
Writing about them one after another, flowing and vanishing lumping layers

Er-long Village, Two dragons one river
Upstream connected to Mi-Lo River,
Year in years out at Dragon Boat Festival, heard is the
Sad songs of a thousand years
Chu-yuan Li-sao, his long grievance poems,
The sound of gongs and drums playing noisily into the skies, as poem offerings for a thousand years

找影子的人

我在夜裡走著；我該更清楚的說，
我自己一個人走著，走在沒有光的夜裡
我是一個沒有影子的人
其實，我還應該更清楚的說
我走在夢裡的黑夜裡的時間的地道裡，
有光，是在不確定的前方；
只有星星點點，我不確定的前方的星星點點
我需要同伴，我只有我一個人
我需要影子，我本來有我自己的影子
但他怕黑，他就不再陪我
留在有光的地方，要我自己孤單的走完
這一趟夢裡的黑夜，因為這是我
自己決定的行程，走向我靈魂失落的故鄉
沒有影子的人，是注定要寂寞孤獨的
和黑夜在一起，而且必須是要醒著的
要自己去面對一切的不確定的未來；
我不能有半點猶豫，我不能有
半點後悔；千真萬確的，
我必須告訴自己，你必須繼續孤單的
走下去，沒有回頭
影子不會在黑夜裡等你——
明白了這就是我的人生，我的宿命
我與自己同行，我找到詩
我看到前方的星星點點，我仍在
夢裡的黑夜裡的時間的地道裡，
我看到自己，與詩同行……

（2017.05.30 詩人節／07:41 研究苑）

He Who Looks for His Own Shadow

I'm walking in the night; I should've been more clear in saying,

I'm alone walking, in the light-less or unlit night

I'm a shadow-less man

In fact, I should've said more clearly

I'm walking in the dark night through the tunnel or underpass of time in a dream

There's a light. It's in front of me at an uncertain or unknown place;

Only there are dots of light and spots of stars; I'm not certain of those spots and stars ahead of me

I need a companion, for it is now only me alone

I need a shadow; I've originally got my own shadow

But it's afraid of darkness, so it won't be with me any more

It remains where there's light, wanting me to walk on by myself to the end

This journey in the dark night in the dream, because it's me

I've decided on taking this journey, walking toward my hometown where my soul's got lost

A man without his shadow, is destined to be lonely feeling alone

Together with the dark night, and must also keep wide awake

I have to face everything uncertain in future on my own

I can't be any bit of hesitating at all, nor any bit of regretting; it's very real, absolutely true,

I must tell myself:You must go on alone and lonely

To walk on, without turning your head back

The shadow won't wait in the dead dark night for you--- ----

Realizing it's my life, my fate

Me, I go with myself alone, I find poetry

I see ahead of me those stars and spots, I'm still

In the dream in the dark night of time tunnel,

I see myself, walking along with poetry

我，什麼都沒有

空氣，不是我的；
我活著，
空氣是我的。

我，抬頭
我可以仰望天空；
我，低頭
我可以注視大地；

謝天謝地，
我，一直都擁有這些
那些；這些那些
都不屬於我的……

（2017.05.31／20:27 在社巴上，到家了！）

Me, I've Got Nothing

Air, it isn't mine;
I'm living,
Then the air is mine.

Me, I raise my head
I can look up at the sky;
Me, I lower my head
I can stare at the great earth

Thank the sky and earth,
Me, I've owned all these
Those; these " those"
All that doesn't belong to me......

夜裡，我打開的一頁

夜裡，是我打開的一本書嗎？
我仰望天際，和白天不一樣
我讀不懂的奧義，都藏在
每一顆星子裡；
你說它小嗎？
每一顆都藏著
億萬光年的距離，我的心事也能放大
億萬光年的倍數
啊！我何曾渺小過，如沙灘上的細沙
任何一粒，我要如何雕它
芒雕我的心事？是我回望我白天打開的
天空，一片晴朗，我的心是透明的；
毫無塵埃，我能坦蕩面對
宇宙，大地，翠綠一片
無一障礙，再多也無人多汽車多，
空氣污染，
政治齷齪，人性貪婪……
我打開的書，最難翻閱的一頁，
月亮不見，星星不見
光害太多，……

（2017.06.02／00:20 研究苑）

In the Night, the One Page I Opened

In the night, is it not that book I opened?

I looked up at the edge of the sky, and it's unlike the broad day time

I couldn't comprehend the secrets, which are hidden

In each star;

You said it's small?

Each star hides

At a distance from a thousand billions of light years away, so my heart secrets also could be multiplied and probably so enlarged as many times.

Ah! How insignificant I've been, like a fine tiny grain of sand on the beach

Any grain of it, how could I carve or sculpt it in a micro weed art project depicting the secrets in my heart? That I open my heart when I look it back in the broad day time.

In the sky, there's a vast expanse of the fine and sky heaven, with my transparent mind of clear conscience;

All's dustless and dust-free where I can openly and freely face the universe

The great earth and the stretch of emerald green

Without any obstacles, which at most are less than the number of people and cars,

Air pollution,

Corrupted and unreliable politics, greedy nature of human beings.......

I opened my book, to that page which is the hardest to turn over to,

The moon is invisible, and the stars are invisible

The light pollution is too much and serious, ...

想想，我的小貓兒

我喜歡坐在靠窗的旁邊，那
是我們家
二樓的客廳；靠窗的旁邊
會有窗外木蘭花高大的樹影，
為我遮涼；我說的是

那是夏天的午後，我坐在大沙發上
像爺爺奶奶抱著我的小時候，
我是窩著的在讀一本書，我讀的是
一個爺爺級的詩人寫的，
有貓有狗，有花和蝴蝶……
他當然還知道我，最喜歡讀的是
詩中有著濃濃的童稚的奶香味；
他常常不小心，就在他的詩裡行間
偷偷地回到了他的童年，也回到了
我更小的童年；像我窩在媽媽懷裡，
這個時候，你知道吧！
是夕陽快要西下時，彩霞會透過
落地玻璃窗，如果有貓兒走過
我還能從地板上發現，
我們家又多了一隻小黑貓；
當然，這只是我想的
否則媽媽會說，一隻就夠了
要是牠們愛打架咱怎麼辦？
是啦！我只是想想而已，
我常常覺得，我自己一個人在家
沒有玩伴的時候
是很無聊的，貓兒也應該要有個伴兒。
真的。我替牠想了，牠也該為我想
當我很無聊的時候，我們就該互相
為對方想想……

（2017.06.07／19:40 研究苑）

Think Hard Once More, My Little Kitten

I like sitting next to the window, that's

My home

The living room on the second floor; beside what's close to the window where

There's the tall big tree shadow of Magnolia, Mu-lan flower tree,

Giving me a shade to cool myself; I want to say

That's an afternoon in summer, I sat on the large long sofa

Like my grandpa and grandma embracing me as a child,

I was snuggling up reading a book,

Written by an author friend of my grandfather's,

Where there are cats and dogs as well as flowers and butterflies.......

He's surely knows me, and what I love reading is

There in the poems exuding the thick and dense milky aromatic smell of the young naive children

He's always careless, right in the written words between the lines of his poems

Sneaking into his childhood, also returning to

My much younger childhood; like me being snuggling up in Mum's chest

At this time, you know what!

It's the moment the setting sun 's sinking into the west, the colorful afterglow of gloaming will go
   piercing

Through the window glass panel from the ceiling, if there's a cat passing

I can also find from what's on the floor,

There's one more little black cat being kept and raised in my home;

Of course, it's only what's I'm thinking about

Otherwise Mum would say, one is enough

Provided they might like fighting each other what should we do?

That's right! I'm just pondering,

I always feel that, me, I'm only myself alone at home

When nobody else is in my company

It's very boring, the cat should also need a company or partner.

Indeed. I'm thinking about this for it; it should also think about this for me.

When I'm very bored, we should

Think hard once more for the other.......

我的小貓不睡覺

我的小貓小小，牠不睡覺
夜深了，
牠只喜歡眯著眼睛；
你以為牠睡著了，
牠是假裝的，牠是在意你
有沒有在陪牠，
有沒有在夢裡，也為牠寫一首
有魚的小詩？

（2017.06.11／09:34 研究苑）

My Little Kitten Doesn't Sleep

My little kitten small and tiny. It doesn't sleep

In the dead darkness of night,

It just likes to squint its eyes;

You mistake it for sleeping,

She's faking and pretending, it actually watching you stealing a look at you

If you're accompanying it,

If you're in your dream, also write it a

Poem featuring s fish?

在夢裡也要想牠

小小的，我的貓，
半夜裡，牠會出走——
害我在夢裡找牠；
我記得牠是上屋頂去，
要找月亮和星星約會；
我告訴牠，城裡燈太亮了
牠說牠會走到最暗的裡邊，
不讓我看到；是的，
牠是黑色的，我忘了
牠是全黑的；牠是故意的，
牠要我在夢裡，也一定要——
要想牠。

（2017.06.11／11:57 研究苑）

Thinking about It Even in My Dream

The little tiny one, my kitten,

In the midnight, it'll go outing—

Giving me troubles trying to find it in the dream;

I remember it climbing onto the house roof,

Wanting to date with the moon and stars,

I told it, the lamps were too light downtown in the city

It said it'd get to the darkest inner site,

Not letting me see it; yes,

It's black, I forget about it

It's the all black the whole body; it's on purpose

It's wanted me even in the dream to have to think about it—

want to think about it.

我看，不見的小貓

黑黑小小，我的小貓
牠越走越遠，就越黑越小了
我還在夜裡看著牠，越走越遠
牠害我一路都在跟蹤牠；
其實這麼辛苦
只要我還能想著就好了。
想著想著，沒有一件事是不想的
我的小貓，小小，黑黑
黑黑，小小
每每一走進夜裡，只要沒有光害
牠就可以安然自在的不見了，
我也就可以安心的
睡著了，我看不見的小貓……

（2017.06.11／14:27 胡思公館店）

Looking around, I Can't to Find My Little Kitten

Dark black, small and cute, my little kitten

It goes farther and farther, thus the black spots are getting smaller and smaller

In the night I'm still looking at it, walking farther and farther

It makes me so many troubles that I have to go after it all the way it goes;

In fact it's such a troublesome thing to do

It'd be OK as long as I can still think about it.

Think it over and over again, there's not anything else I can't think about

My little kitten, small and cute, dark and black

Dark and black, little and cute

Every time entering the night, if only there's no light pollution

It can be out of sight feeling carefree at ease and peaceful

Me, too I can feel carefree

When sleeping, I am unable to see my little kitten

貓，牠不講理
──我的貓小小，其實牠一點也不小

從一開始牠就懂得如何抓住
我的耳朵，我的腦袋，我的心
當牠在我耳朵裡的時候，
我只有聽牠的喵喵喵的撒嬌；
當牠跳進我的腦海裡，
我只好開始想牠的好的種種好；
當牠鑽進我的心窩裡，我也只好認了
任牠乖乖窩著，纏纏綿綿
夜夜纏綿；我是完全沒有意見的了，
但更多的時候，我也不敢想牠
牠也照樣如此如此，
揮之不去，那種意思
你當了解，作為我的貓，
牠小小，牠真的一點也不小
牠，
霸佔了我的耳朵，
霸佔了我的腦海，
霸佔了我的整顆，軟綿綿的
整顆的心！

（2017.06.11／22:03 研究苑）

The Irreasonable Kitten;
in Fact, It's Not Small at all

From the beginning, it knew how to catch my ears, my head and my heart

When it's biting my ears,

I just hear her meow, meow to please and flirt me;

When it jumps into my head,

I can only ponder all its good and kindness;

When it sneaks entering my heart, I've got no choice but take it

Allowing it nicely coils, cuddling lingering around me

Lingering every night; I've got nothing to say,

But the more of my time I dare not think about it

It does what's done so all the same,

Unable to be get rid of

You must know that, be a kitten of mine,

It little and small, it indeed isn't small at all

It,

Forcibly occupies and take over my ears,

Forcibly occupies and take over my head and mind

Forcibly occupies and take over the whole softened heart of mine,

牠，只喵兩聲

小小，黑黑，我的貓是有智慧的
牠告訴我，已經不再是我告訴牠；
牠說：人要懂得禮貌和是非。
這是我以前告訴過牠的，我當然是說：
貓要懂得禮貌和是非。
不錯！就因為牠懂，我才尊重牠。
有一天，應該說
有一個晚上，牠坐在我的閱讀的檯燈下
牠看我看我自己的書；
那是我寫的
貓詩。牠說，只喵兩聲，不屑的
就不再理我了！

我知道，自己寫的
那有什麼好看？

這是很傷的；我只是因為我剛收到的
一本新書，總該檢查一下嘛
也包括滿足自我陶醉，就這麼一點點虛榮
牠就不舒服，最好是
我應該首先把牠摟在懷裡，然後
再開始愛怎麼陶醉自己就怎麼陶醉吧！
其實，我的貓小小，黑黑
牠的心，也還是黑黑，小小
容不下我一開始說的，牠是有智慧的
那麼一點點優點！

（2017.06.13／07:17 研究苑）

It, Just Makes Two Mew Sounds

Little and small, black and dark, my kitten is a wise smart cat.

It tells me, it's no longer what I have been told about it;

It says: Humans must be polite and tell right from wrong.

This is what I told to the cat before; I'd certainly said this before:

Cats must be polite to others and tell right from wrong.

That's right! Just because it understands this, so I respect it.

Some day, I should say

One night, it sat under my reading lamp

It saw me reading the book I've written;

That's what I wrote

Entitled Poems on Cats. It says, just giving two mew sounds eying me down in a disdaining look

Then caring me not a bit!

I know it, my own writing

What's the hell worthy the reading?

It hurts me a lot; I just feel so because I've just got it.

A brand-new book, it should be checked somehow, right?

Also including satisfying my self-contentedness or indulging, just a little bit of vanity

It doesn't feel good, the best thing I can do would be that

I should've first embraced it in my chest,

Again starting to indulge in whatever self-contentedness I'd like to enjoy doing

In fact, my kitten so little and cute, also dark and black, so is its heart black and dark, small and cute as
  not to comply with what I've said in the beginning; it's a wise and smart cat

That's a little bit of its strength and advantage!

說說好的，我的貓

今晚，我的貓跟我說好
約法三章——
牠可以睡牠的覺，
我可以
睡我自己的；說說好的，
但未必都要能做到，比如
昨天以前的昨天，
就是前天，也是牠先說的
你不要在夢裡為我寫詩，
我還是
在夢裡，為牠寫詩。

是的。說說好的，睡覺之前，
我們都約好，說好
為什麼今天早上我醒來，
你，我的小貓，貓小小的
你怎麼還是
窩在我的棉被裡？

（2017.06.14／03:12 研究苑）

It's Just What I've Ruled, My Kitten

Tonight, my kitten promised what I've told it.

A set of rules between us two

It can sleep how it may

I can sleep my own way; it's s deal between us,

But we can't make it to keep the word, for example

The yesterday before yesterday,

That's two days ago, also what it first said

You don't write me poems in the dream,

I'm still

In the dream, writing her poems.

Yes, it's a promise and you word to keep

We both made the promise, by saying

Why this morning today when I woke up

You. My little small cat, while you're still cat small and little

Snuggling up in my cotton bed sheets and coverings?

我的貓是自由的

常常進出我腦海中的那隻
小貓，牠是我的
但我都不必費心飼養；
牠是自由的，我的貓百分之一百
隨時可進出我的腦海，
我沒有限制牠；從我年輕開始──
我是崇尚自由的，
我也尊重我的貓，我一直記住
牠的好，當然，我也知道牠的壞；
其實，誰沒有壞？
牠壞在哪兒？就是我不想牠的時候，
牠也會自動跑進我的腦海，
其實，更準確的說，
牠也不是用跑的；牠，向來
走路是沒有聲音的，
躡足躡腳，比雲還輕
所以，在我夢裡牠也照樣
可以自由進出我的腦海，
再深的腦海也一樣，
對牠都不是問題，有問題的
還是我，誰叫我半夜裡
也還要想牠？
已逾半個世紀了，我也還在想牠
我的貓小小，小小
黑黑，就是我的貓。

（2017.06.16／03:28 研究苑）

My Kitten is Free

It's the one that often flashes across my mind, getting inside and out of it,

The little kitten, it's mine

But I don't need to make efforts to feed it;

It's free, my kitten's one hundred percent free totally

Anytime, it can enter and go out of my mind

I've never controlled, limited it or placed any restrictions on it; since I was young—

I highly regarded my freedom and pursued a free lifestyle.,

I also pay high respect for my kitten; I've always kept it in my mind.

It's good, of course, I also know he's bad, that is, naughty or mischievous or disobedient;

In fact, who's not sometimes bad, evil or devious while going through his rebellious stage?

When and where it's evil or devilish? It's when and where I'm not thinking of it or out of my mind.

It can also automatically flash or cross my mind; that is just runs into it.

In fact, to be more exact,

It's not born for running; it has always been walking without making any noise,

Tiptoeing, stepping more lightly than like drifting in the cloud

So, in my dream it can also

Enter and get out of my mind,

Even in the innermost bottom of the mind or my heart

There's not any problem with it, the problem is

With me, for it's me who even at midnight,

Am still thinking about it.

For more than a half century, I've been still thinking about it

My little small, little cute kitten

Dark and black, it's my kitten.

我的貓的高度

　　　　貓，坐著比站著高。（王玉川兒歌）

貓有高度，我的貓的高度
不是平常走路時的高度；當然，
牠坐著的時候，比走來走去時
還要高許多。
所以，
牠喜歡坐著；
當然，我要說的是
我的貓的高度是，比牠坐著的時候
還要高——
那高度，就是牠坐著的時候
牠在想，牠是詩人
牠是思想家，
牠是哲學家，
牠也是宗教家……

你看過嗎？
其實，牠什麼都不是
這個時候，牠都不理人
我想，牠還是關心
海裡有沒有魚，
海裡有那麼多的垃圾，
今天的魚，還好嗎？

（2017.06.16／09:26 研究苑）

My Kitten in Its Height at a High Altitude

The cat, is taller when it's sitting than when standing

—from Children's song by Wang, Yu-chuan

A cat can draw itself up to its full height, so my kitten has got its height, at a higher altitude.

It's not the height it maintains when walking; certainly,

When sitting, it's relatively seated much higher than

While walking or wandering or loitering or hanging around here and there.

Therefore,

It likes sitting;

Of course, what I want to say is

My kitten gains its greater height, which looks much taller, when it's in the sitting position or posture

In a towering height—

That height, is to be attained when sitting, of thinking of itself to be a poet

It's a great thinker,

It's a talent philosopher,

It's also a faithful and religious leader......

Have you ever seen it?

As a matter of fact, it's none of them all.

At this moment, I think it's still concerned and worried about

Whether there's any fish at sea or not

Whether there's that much trash thrown into the sea, or not

Today's fish, are they still fine in there, OK?

我的貓是幸福的

今天有魚，餐餐
都有魚；我的貓，
我沒有養牠，牠只管靜靜地
坐著，
在我腦海中坐著，
用我的眼睛
專注的看著我在吃魚；
今天下雨，昨天下雨
前天下雨，大前天也在下雨……
我的貓很安靜，牠只對著窗外看
豪雨之後，那不就是一片汪洋嗎?!
每一根從天而降的雨絲，不就是
一種垂釣？
魚竿呢？
魚呢？

牠不小心回過頭來，牠看到我──
怎麼屋裡也要養魚
？？？？？？

（2017.06.16／12:44 研究苑）

My Lucky and Happy Kitten

Today there is fish served to feed it, all the meals

All with fish included; my dear kitten,

I don't spoon-feed it, so it's just quietly

Sitting over there,

In my mind, being seated just right there,

Using my eyes

Concentrating on staring at me eating fish;

Today it's raining, and yesterday's raining

It's raining the other day; it's keeping raining, so was the day before yesterday

My kitten is so quiet and calm, looking at and out of the window

After the heavy downpour, is that the vast boundless expanse of surging and raging waves being formed?!

Each silk-like thread line of rain coming falling from the sky,

Isn't it like an act of dropping fishing rods?

How about the fishing pole?

and my fish?

Carelessly it is inadvertently looking back, yet not cautiously enough to see me over there

Why should the fish also be being fed, raised and kept in the house.

? ? ? ? ? ?

我陪牠，把夜熬爛

一夜，我已醒來三次，
這也表示，我已睡過三回；
說一夜，其實也不準確
才剛剛過了凌晨三點，
還有難熬的下半夜——
都是蚊子害的，我的貓不知道
我沒有告訴牠
牠不會知道；不管牠有沒有睡，
反正牠是閉著眼，也無一點動靜
幸福，就在什麼都可以不管
什麼都不用操心；牠有句名言
黑夜來了，只要閉上眼
就沒事了！
其他動物、昆蟲，除了蚊子
似乎大家都聽牠的，
這個夜就真的這麼安靜了？
不，我最慘，蚊子一直找我
我必須陪牠，把夜熬爛！

（2017.06.16／16:37 胡思公館店）

Enjoy Being with It Burning the Midnight's Oil till out of Gasoline

The whole night, I'd been awoken three times,

That means, I'd been slept three rounds;

In fact it's not exactly one round of sleep overnight

It's past three o'clock in the early morning,

There still remaining the second half of the midnight to endure-----

The harmful mosquitoes were to blame; yet my kitten has no idea of what happened

I didn't tell anything about it to my cat

It won't know that; no matter it had been sleeping or not,

At any rate all I know is that it'd been closing its eyes, staying there still and static

Happiness, is like this: there's not anything at all that needs you to care about whatever may get you to be
　concerned; that's a famous saying of, or words of wisdom

When night falls, just close your eyes and

Then there's nothing else to care or worry about

All the other animals, insects, except mosquitoes,

They seem to have taken and heed its advice

Thus, this night indeed is this quiet and silent?

No. I'm the most miserable and pitiful one, because the mosquitoes had kept biting me

I had no choice but accompany it, to go it alone out throughout the torture in the entire night until the
　night ends!

我們都知道

天晴真好。我的貓說；
雨天，牠在我心裡，
晴天，牠也在我腦海中
牠會為我想，也會為我
擔心。
豪雨過了嗎？今天，明天？
據說後天才會緩和；我的屋漏，
是屋裡的尼加拉瓜，有時也是
十分寮瀑布！！！！！！
屋漏的事，七十年前
小小的時候，我就懂
杓盆碗盤，再大的甕也要出動
接我們全家的心聲；
我的小小的貓，牠透過我的腦海和眼睛
也能清楚看到，
牠知道，這是我的一輩子的苦
前世帶來今生
小小的，我心中的貓
牠貼著我的心，牠知道我心跳
牠也知道，這與牠有關；牠和我
也是，前世今生
我們都這樣想著
晴天，真好
希望別再有豪雨。

（2017.06.18／10:30 捷運板南線忠孝敦化）

We Both Know That

"It's fine; that's really great," says my kitten;

In rainy days, it's in my mind,

In fine weather, it's in my mind

It'll think for me as it's not only in my shoes; it's also worried about and

Concerned with me

Is the heavy downpour gone? Today, tomorrow?

It's said that the day after tomorrow it'll get better, finer and more pleasant and agreeable; the leakage
  problem with my house so grave and acute

In the house it's like the Niagara Falls; sometimes it is

Like the Shi Fen Liao Falls in Shuang-xi in the hilly countryside of New Taipei City

The troubling problems with house leakage, started seventy years ago

When very young, I've experienced to fully realize that

Ladles, basins, bowls and, dishes, even those much larger vases, all need to be mobilized to be taken out
  to serve for taking in the raining drops and waters meanwhile

Also taking in the innermost heart voice from the hearts of my whole family;

My little small kitten, through my brain and mind's eye

That can see all these clearly,

It knows, this it's my pains, sufferings and bitterness witnessed and experienced by me the whole life

Its previous life bringing me into and carried me on into this life.

The little small petty thing, that's the kitten remains in my mind

It gets close to the innermost bottom of my heart, feeling my heart beating throbbing and thrilling

It also knows, this has something to do with my kitten□both of us two.

Also, it's our previous generation as well as this life, also this very generation

We all ponder on that this way

A good fine weather now, this is indeed great and superb

We both hope there won't be any heavy downpour.

我罵牠睡貓

睜一眼閉一眼，我的貓做到了！
我的貓，牠知道
我有什麼缺點，什麼毛病
心照不宣；誰沒有毛病，
誰不偷偷偷懶？這是牠說的
不可告人的名言；
是的。我和牠有良好的默契，
我們常常在夢裡交換祕密；比如
牠喜歡吃魚，我也喜歡吃魚
牠安慰我，你不一定要變成貓
我也常常告訴牠，你也不必變成人
當人是很累的呢！
是的。我們都很要好，正因為
我們可以這樣交心；
我也懂得賄賂牠，我會在夢中
給牠很多好處，要魚有魚
所以，我偶爾會做點壞事——
背叛牠，偷偷自己在夢醒時
罵牠
牠也照樣，睜一眼閉一眼
甚至搗著耳朵，假裝沒聽見；
還好。我罵牠睡貓
懶得捉老鼠的——
真實的壞話。

（2017.06.21／16:29 歷史博物館）

I Scolded, Cursed My Kitten,
"A Snoozing Sleepyhead! "

With one eye closed and another wide open, my kitten made it!

My kitten knows it well how

I've got some shortcomings, some bad habits or weaknesses,

We have a tacit, mutual understanding of who doesn't have any weaknesses

Who won't skulk or shirk from work in a sneak, secret way? That's the wise words that it's said about
  untold to others.

Yes. Me and it have good consensus or tacit understanding,

We often exchange secrets in our dreams: for example,

It likes fishes, and so do I, as it consoles me, saying "You don't need to make yourself a kitten like me."

I always tell it, too, "You don't need to make yourself a human either."

Being a human being is a tiresome and boring thing!

Yes. We are all well. Be ourselves! Just because

We can talk and chat heart to heart like this;

I also know how to bribe it; I'll do that in my dream

Giving it a lot of favors, "You want fish, get the fish you desire—

So, I sometimes do things a little bit devilish or evil—

Betray it, speak ill of it and curse or abuse it behind its back

as usual it still keeps one eye wide open and another closed down into even covering its ears pretending
  not to hear

That's OK. I curse or scold it by calling it as a sleepyhead kitten, too lazy to catch mice—

That's the true ills I speak of or badmouth my kitten.

我沒跟牠約定

牠固定會坐在窗前，以牠習慣坐著的
高度，向窗外張望
這個時候，應該說有幾分薄暮
有時會有幾隻鳥兒飛過，不確定
牠們該叫
什麼鳥？大多是灰黑色，
與暮色幾無差別
我的貓，主要應該是要等我
但也不能確定，
我沒跟牠約好，自然談不上準不準時；
沒有約定也等於約定，
彷彿只要我該回來我就回來，只是
每回我回來的時候，
牠都守在那裡，假裝
牠不是在等我
被等待或等待人家，其實都很累
我常常告訴牠，我會回來
你用不著坐在窗前苦苦的等；
太陽和月亮，也從來沒有誰要等誰。

（2017.06.19／21:37 研究苑）

I've Not Made Any Date with My Kitten Yet

It sits as usual in front of the window, in its habitual posture

At its greatest height, looking out of the window seeing around

At this moment, there should be somewhat in the thin fog.

Sometimes there will be several birds flying over getting across, uncertain or not sure

If they be crowing chirping and shouting

What birds? Most of them are graying dark,

Exactly close to the color of gloaming afterglow twilight almost with no difference.

My kitten, chiefly there waiting for me

But I'm not sure, either,

I haven't made a date with it, naturally it's nothing about being on time or not;

No dating is the same as having a date

It seems as long as it's time for me to come back,

Just that each time I come back,

The kitten is there watching over, pretending

It's not waiting for me

Either being waited for or waiting for others, in fact, both are tiresome and boring

I often tell my kitten, I'll come back

You don't need the bother of sitting in front of the window making such bitter efforts longing for my
 return;

The sun and the moon, either is never waiting for any other.

牠，走來走去

午休時，我的貓也眯著眼
在我腦海中，陪伴我；

我在想，我忍了很久該不該問我自己，我是貓嗎
為什麼我要這樣懷疑？
我幾乎天天都吃魚，
也許我是貓的後裔；
當我吃魚的時候，我會想到
我的貓，牠在我腦海中
有沒有魚吃？我這樣想牠的時候，
我也會想到海，當然也想到魚
海不就是魚的家嗎？

我繼續想，想得很多很深的時候
我就真的睡著了
但牠，還是走來走去
在我腦海裡……

（2017.06.23／14:36 研究苑）

It Comes and Goes, Walking Here and There

At noon taking a nap, my kitten also squinting its eyes
Appearing in my mind, being around with me;

I'm just thinking, I've stood and tolerated it for quite a long time
Should I ask myself, am I a kitten, too?
Why should I doubt this?
I almost eat fish every day,
Maybe I'm a descendent or offspring of a kitten;
When I eat fish, I'll think of
My kitten, it's in my mind
Any fish for me to eat? As I'm so much thinking of it?
I'll also think of the sea, of course, of fish at the same time
Isn't the sea home to the fish?

I kept on pondering, falling into many thoughts rather deeply.
Then I fell truly asleep so soundly
But the kitten, still walking around here and there loitering
In my mind and my brain……

牠告訴我

我愛睡的貓，牠告訴我
牠已經學會了睡覺時
一定要打呼，讓鼾聲充滿
整個寢室，那是一種
幸福。

我常常半夜起來，偷偷看牠
瞄牠；
牠，有沒有
騙我？偶爾被騙了，
自己也感覺有那麼一點點幸福的感覺，
要不，為什麼要苦苦
在半夜起床？
其實，如果能夠一覺到天亮
那該多好呀！
我的貓反問我說：

你有嗎，那一覺到天亮？

（2017.06.26／13:02 研究苑）

It Told Me That

The sleep-loving kitten of mine, when it told me that
It had already learned to sleep when
It would surely snooze, with its snoozing noise filling
The whole bedroom, that is, a feeling of happiness,

I often wake in the midnight to squint at it
Hasn't it
Told a lie to me? I'm sometimes cheated
I also feel that little sense of happiness,
Otherwise. Why should I take pain to get up in the midnight?
In fact, if I could have slept soundly the whole night till daybreak,
How great that would be?
My kitten asked me back in reply:

Have you, also slept soundly till daybreak?

我們在海邊

現在我要去海邊，一個
淺水灣的海邊；在三芝，
那裡靠近海，
今天有陽光，那裡有沙灘，
沙灘之外就是海；
海是魚的家，一定有魚。
我把我的貓，也一起帶著走
到海邊，在淺水灣
讓牠看看海，看看海有多大
牠在我的腦海中，牠可以發揮想像
想海有多大就有多大！
我有一頭白髮，又把白髮
養長了！海邊有風，
愛沉思冥想的我，坐在臨海的窗邊
讓我的貓看在牠眼裡，牠也該學著我
長坐冥想；我不知牠是否已經入神
得道否，是否已經入禪
有風吹不動了，我知道
我們都已經完全神話了！

（2017.06.26／00:23 研究苑）

We're at the Seaside

Now I'm going to the seashore, the seaside
Next to the Qian-shui or Shallow Bay; at San Chi(San-zhi), Tam-shui
Over there it's near the sea,
Today there's the sunshine; here's the sand beach,
Beyond the seaside is the sea;
The sea is home to fish, where there must be fish.
I take my kitten, walking together
To the seashore, in the Shallow Bay
Letting it have a look at the sea, seeing how huge it is
It's in my mind; it can exercise its imagination
Pondering how big it is and it's as farther as it's thoughts or imagination can reach
I've got a full-head of white hair, and also have the white hair
Grown up long!
There's a breeze at the seaside,
Me, the meditation lover, sitting beside the window that is next to the sea
Letting my kitten as it looks at me should learn from me
Sitting long enough to meditate; I'm wondering if it has learned to sink down into a trance
If it's already got enlightened; whether it's already practiced entering the realm of Zen
So quiet and firm yet the wind can't move it a bit. I know
Both of us have already been entirely in a legendary myth!

牠不欠我

我常常仰望夜晚
沒有星星沒有月亮的天空，
在空無一人的我自己的心上；
這個時候，我有我的貓在陪我
也可以說我在陪牠……
在自己心裡，這是很自在的
對誰都沒有虧欠；
從前世到今生，
從人到貓，或從貓到人
都無從分辨，
我安於孤寂，無所期求
我的貓，牠不欠我
我也不欠牠；牠願意陪我，
接受孤寂
我，常常發呆
自認為自己得到了，其實
更多的，包括時間
都一一流失，我也成為
時間的一部分……

（2017.06.27／21:06 研究苑）

It Owes Me Nothing

I'm always looking up at the night sky

Where no stars is visible and the moon is out of sight in the sky.

In my own heart there is no one else;

At this moment, I've got my kitten to be together at my side

I may as well say I'm having the kitten around next to me.......

In my own heart, it feels so carefree and at ease without each one owning any part of anything of the
   other;

From the previous life to this life,

From a man to a cat, or vice versa from cats to men, it's unlikely to discern or tell the difference.

I settle in my loneliness, expecting nothing

Neither does my kitten owe me any part or anything

I don't owe it anything; she's willing to accompany me,

Taking my loneliness for granted

Me, I'll be often sunk in a trance mediating

I also think of myself I've got something; in fact

Getting more than that, including time.

That's going to lose one by one, me I've also turned as

A Part of time......

我們雞同鴨講

天下的事都很奇怪，
生肖兔子
又是獅子座的我，我的有智慧的貓
牠總認為我是不應該
成為詩人的！
那要成為什麼？
我問牠，牠說我缺少智慧
只能做一個乖乖牌的隨從，
跟在牠背後就好了！
根據十二星座的貓來看，
一樣具有高貴氣質的我，
我應該足可和我的雙魚座的貓，
平起平坐，不只可以寫詩
甚至也可以有特權，當貴族
什麼事都可以不用做。
愛流浪的我的雙魚座的貓，
牠總有一份自信，自以為是
牠說了算
作為獅子座的我
我是很沒面子的；我真不懂牠在想什麼，
牠也真的很不懂得我要說的是什麼？
雞同鴨講！
至於我們都是詩人，我早早就說過
此一特質，我們還是要好好保存著
做做樣子，每天寫一首壞詩
也很不錯！是的，我就這麼認為
我很不錯！

（2017.06.29／06:55 研究苑）

We Chickens Can't Talk with Ducks

In the human world everything is so strange,

In the Chinese zodiac signs I was born in the year of the rabbit or hare

Also a lion in the horoscope, but my wisdom is just that of a cat

It always thinks of me not entitled

To be a poet!

Then what am I supposed to be?

I asked it, with its answer: I'm, in short of wisdom,

I'm just good for being an obedient attendant

Just following its footsteps!

According to the twelve zodiac signs,

Like the kitten,

I have the same inclination of a noble-status man,

I should be equal to the kitten of a Pieces sign

On the same tandem, I'm not only able to write poems,

But also to wield my authority, as a noble man entitled to do nothing common or ordinary.

My Pieces sign kitten Who loves wandering a lot,

It's always full of self-confidence, being very self-conceited or assertive or decisive

As that of a Leon sign

I'm losing my face; indeed I don't know what's in its mind,

It's in reality doesn't understand what I'm going to say?

A case of a chicken being talking with a duck! Not on a par of or keep sensible communication.

As regards we both being poets, that I talked about long, long ago

With such a characteristic feature we've got to maintain

Faking or pretending to be one, by writing a bad poem a day,

That's not bad! Yes, I think so.

I'm indeed superb!

我做夢也在想

我的貓，通常對我都沒有意見
牠不用我養，牠不吃任何食物
永遠都不餓；但牠在意什麼？
牠滿計較，常常問我
有沒有想牠？
我說我有想，牠說這樣還不夠
要24小時都在想。這怎麼可能！
牠說，就是要這樣，
否則就不算想！
那睡覺的時候呢？
也要。牠很肯定的說，
做夢也要。做夢？
我說有，你說沒有
那怎麼辦！我們因此而常常吵架。
牠說吵吵架，這樣才好玩；
不吵就不好玩。
我的貓，就這麼怪，不吃東西
就要我常常餵牠想；騙牠想，
騙牠我做夢也在想──

（2017.06.30／12:22 研究苑）

I'm Thinking Even in the Dreams

My kitten, generally has no opinions on me

It doesn't want me to feed it, nor does it feed on any food

It's never feeling hungry; yet what does it care about?

It cares a lot and it's particular about something, always keep asking me

Am I thinking about it?

I say I'm. It says that's not enough.

I must think about it. How could it be possible? twenty-four hours

It says, that's it,

Otherwise it's not about genuinely thinking about!

Then what's about sleeping time?

Also included. It responds definitely yes,

Even in your dream. Dreaming?

I say yes I'm, but you say no.

Well, what should we do! For this we squabble and argue a lot.

It said such squabbling and arguing would be good; it's a lot of fun. No squabbling no fun.

My cat that's such queer and weird; don't eat anything

Just wanting me always feed it; cheat it to think

Deceiving that I'm thinking even when I'm dreaming.

戲和那年夏天
——致王渝

今夏到來，先是豪雨
打亂了植物園那道旋轉的門，
也絞亂了旅人的心緒；那年，
不在的那年，
遠走的豈只是一個人
一個人，一顆心
帶走了整個三月、四月、五月
的美好！

久違了！時間的殤逝，美好的
季節的容顏，
回首都在雲霧中，那春天走過的田野
那年少走過的校園，那朗朗的
詩聲，朗朗的笑語
那一陣陣豪雨，打亂了那個夏季
植物園的荷塘翠綠，
今夏依舊擎起，夢中一片
激動的紅暈……

（2017.07.02／04:29 研究苑）

Poem Echoing "That Summer"
—To WANG Yu

This summer arrived, first with a downpour shower

Messing up that revolving door at the entrance of the Taipei Botanical Garden on Nan Hai Road

Also twisting and confusing the heart and mood of a traveler; that year,

That year you're absent,

Going to a faraway place it couldn't be just only one person

a heart for an individual,

Being carried away what's all the beautiful experiences in the whole months of Match, April, May!

Long time no see! The passing away of time, all the beautiful look

Of the season,

When looking back in the cloud and mist, that spring was walking in all the fields and wilderness

That year across the campus we used to walk as teenagers, harking those reading-out-loud moments

  eloquent and clarion poems, and chuckling jokes and whispers

Those gusts of downpour showers, messing up that summer

The greening of the lotus flower pond in the Botanical Garden

This sumner there still holding up, a streth of red halo

That got excited in the dream

夏日，日正當中

要是有人不相信，我站在日正當中
夏天就會起火；我已經安於燃燒，
一種熄不了的怒吼，發自內心最冷的冰山
還能再冷，再冷就不冷了嘛！
我們一而再，再而三
無非證明夏天的寫實，是
畢卡索的寫真
誰還在乎我一定要左右豐滿？
左邊是馬，右邊是羊
我就能和馬蒂斯對話；
誰能質疑我和夏加爾的
裙帶曖昧的關係？
火熱的，夏日的正午
太陽不正當的熱情，有空調調控
不被規範的，不被接受的，
總之，日正當中
我們單純的簡單的關係，
可重新從寬認定……

（2017.07.05／18:51 研究苑）

In the Heat Summertime,
the Burning Sun's High in the Sky

Believe it or not, I'm right and the now standing right under the sun

In the summertime it'll catch fire; I'm ready for staying burning,

A kind of roaring from anger that can't be quenched, put out, coming from the most icy iceberg

It can be even colder, much colder until it's no more or no longer cold at all .

We again and over again, at the third time, just wanting to prove the reality of the blazing summer heat to be

The real work by Picasso

Who still cares for me that I must dominate the richness and bountifulness

On the left there's an horse, on the right side it's a goat

I can go start a dialogue with Matisse;

Who can challenge me for Marc Chagall

In my ambiguous or vague nepotism

relationship with Chagall

Fire burning and scorching, the high noon in the heated summer

The abnormal passion of the sun, which is moderated by the air conditioner

Not disciplined and regulated, not acceptable

In sum, as the sun is right over the head

Our simple pure relationship,

Can be redefined and more flexibly recognized with a definition expanded........

貓，應該有的

貓，應該有的
尊嚴，牠都有；
牠是我的貓，
我是聽牠的，不是牠
聽我
牠，很鴨霸
寧可一輩子都不吃任何食物，
就一定要我，一定要想牠；
想牠，不是一下下
要常常想，要隨時隨地
我常常跟牠說，你這樣
就沒有尊嚴；牠說，
錯了！就要讓人想
才有尊嚴。反過來就什麼都沒有，
我就沒有，我就得一定要
聽牠的
我的貓，牠很堅持
牠說，能堅持這一點
我就什麼都有了！
我就一輩子都給牠
這一點；這一點點點……

（2017.07.06／19:34 在昆陽等回山區的社巴）

What the Kitten Is Supposed to Have

The kitten, what's it supposed to have

It's got to have, including Dignity;

It's my kitten,

I'm listening to it, not the other way round

It is very domineering

I would rather eat nothing at all the whole life

And it's wanted me, so that I must be thinking about it;

Thinking about it. Not just a little while

I must often do so, anytime anywhere

I often tell it by saying, you are such and such

It's not a dignified way; it replied,

Enough, forget about it! You must let others think about you to have the dignity. On the contrary, there's
  nothing left with you,

I have no dignity I definitely have to listen to it.

My kitten, which is insistent on it.

It said, being able to insist on this point

I've got everything already!

I'll offer it this whole life of mine

This point; just this point, a little bit of this point......

早安・日出東方

想，沒有二心的想分心，
我出走也能把牠帶在心上；

早安。日出東方，
東方，就在台東；
我的貓，跟我在一起
昨晚，我們可能都睡得很甜
很放心；今天一大早，
大地剛要睜開眼睛，
我們也同時透過窗戶
看到太陽正從海上升起，
我和我的貓
在都蘭卑南聖地
無時無刻，仰望深邃湛藍繁星
與繆斯對話，與聖靈同在
想，我的貓的想，我和我的貓很專注
在黑夜裡都很專注，
凝視

（2017.07.10／08:55 寫於405 次自強號列車，車過我家鄉）

Good Morning - the Sunrise in the East

Thinking that, there's no single-hearted one thinking of distracting to divide the heart into two.

Whenever I go outing I take it along with me right in my heart;

Good morning. The sun rises in the east, right in Tai-tong;

My kitten, going with me together

Last night, we might be sleeping very soundly with sweet dreams

Very relaxed and carefree: So today very early in the morning,

The great earth's just going to open its eyes,

We at the same time look out to see through the window

Seeing the sun's rising from the sea,

Me and my kitten

We both at the holy place of Du Land of the Bei Nam tribe

Every time at any moment, looking up at the faraway deep azure sky for the multifarious stars

Talking with Muses, staying with holy spirit being present together with us

Thinking that my kitten is thinking; me and my kitten are very absorbed and concentrating

In the dark night, we both are very much focusing,

On gazing at what's in front of us two

有音樂，很輕

音樂，很輕
我在胡思；這兒是書店，
真的胡思也無妨，我的貓牠和我
都已習慣，在這兒
我們一起看書，讀詩，音樂很輕
夏日這樣就接近清涼。
常常，我的貓，我帶牠來
牠眯著該眯的眼睛，
不一定要睡著，最好只是假寐
最好只是單純的陪我，
我為牠寫詩
不是牠愛黏我，
也不是我
愛黏牠；是我們彼此黏著，
夏日嘛！有音樂，有詩
有你和牠，多好！

（2017.07.10／15:20 胡思二手書店）

There's Light Music, So Soft and Tender

The light music, very soft and tender

It's in Hu's second-hand bookstore,

Indeed it's OK on entertaining with confused, foolish thoughts having wild ideas of all sorts as the name

　suggests, me and my kitten we

Both are used to being here

We read books and poems together, over very light music playing in the background

In the summertime we're getting so close to fresh and cool places.

Very often, my kitten, as ring it along here and it squints its eyes,

Not necessarily going to sleep, better just take a nap

Better just simply accompany me

I write poems for it

It's not because it loves to stick to me,

Neither do I so

Loving to sticking it; that's us who stick to each other,

In the summertime! There's music, poetry

There are you and the kitten, how wonderful it is!

你是我的，貓說

世界是我的。我每天都想望世界
希望會變得更好；我的貓也說，
你是我的，希望你每天都想我
不要有別的其他的，亂想
午睡剛剛醒來，太陽是夠大的
祂能照耀著整個世界，整個世界
就屬於祂；我該向祂學習，
我的貓呢？牠太自私了，
牠佔有我，我就成為牠的
小小的，只適合放在牠心裡
想牠；想牠的好，想牠的壞
想一隻貓怎麼能夠統攝
一個人的思想？

一個人究竟
該成為什麼樣的一個人？
世界是我的。你憑什麼這麼肯定的說，
這麼說就能肯定這世界就是你的？
我的貓和我是一樣的幼稚，無知
我們都活在我們自己的
無知的夢想裡！

（2017.07.13／15:10 在下山的社巴上）

You're Mine, Says My Kitten

The world is mine. Everyday I'm longing for the world for which

I'm hoping it'll get better; my kitten also says so,

You're mine, hoping you're thinking about me everyday

Don't have anything else, that is confused and messing up thinking

Just awoke from my afternoon nap, it feels the sun is high and big enough

He can shine the whole world, the entire globe

It belongs to HIM; I should learn from HIM

How about my kitten? It's too selfish,

It occupies and dominates me, thus making me a part of him

A small part of his, so little as only to be put in its heart

Thinking about all its good points and strengths, and about its bad points or shortcomings

Thinking about how a kitten could domineer the thoughts of a person?

A person on the earth should become what kind of person?

The world is mine. What on earth makes you say so firmly and positively?

How come by saying so you can claim the world to be yours?

My kitten as well as me are both childish and naive and innocent

We both are living in our own innocent thoughts and naive dream!

明白不明白的

我遊走在一座城市。我說
我一個人，我還有一隻貓
陪我；
牠躲在我心裡，
不吵不鬧，只要我想牠
誰是適合想誰的？這世界，
只要有人想你，你就是幸福的
只是你不一定知道，
我想你，我不會告訴你
因此，所以
所以我永遠不知道你在想誰？
我只是天天都在掛念，
有一天，我們會明白不明白的
永遠都在
我遊走在一座城市，我的貓
常常關注我，提醒我
凡有陽光的地方，就要避開
聲音，孤寂才不被嚇跑
聽要聽沒有聲音的聲音，看要看
沒有形體的光影，
我謹記在心；我為我的貓遊走
在一個虛擬的時空，那裡只剩
你和我……

（2017.07.13／16:37 胡思公館店）

To Understand What I Don't Understand

I'm wandering in a city. I'd say

I'm by myself being alone, with a kitten

Being around with me

It's hidden in my heart

Making not any noises nor any troubles, just wanting me to think about it

Who suits or accommodates most whom? In this world, as long as someone thinks about you, you're so
  fortunate and lucky.

But you're not necessaryily aware of it,

I'm thinking about you, and I won't tell you so

Therefore,

So I never know whom you're thinking about?

I'm just thinking about you every day,

Someday, we'll understand what we don't understand

We're forever

Wandering in a city, my kitten

Always cares about me, reminding me of

Anywhcre there's the sunshine, we must avoid

The noise lest we should be scared away loneliness and serenity or solitude.

Hearing what's made no noise, seeing what's had

No physical body of light and shadow,

I bear this in mind; I walk and wander for my kitten

In a virtual time and space, where there's only left

You and me......

那把椅子空著
——致諾貝爾和平獎得主劉曉波

民主・自由・生命・和平

那把椅子空著，將永遠空著
只寫一個人的名字

劉曉波

（2017.07.14／09:19 研究苑／聞劉曉波13 日17:35 病逝於瀋陽）

That Empty Chair
—to The Nobel Prize Winner Liu Xiao-po

Democracy. Freedom. Life. Peace

That chair's empty; it'll be empty with only a man's name left

That is

Liu Xiao-po

其實，我沒有

月亮也有脾氣。誰能沒有？
初一十五，都不一樣；我有，
我的貓，也有
我們不常犯盲，
有時也愛
耍一點點，我不理牠
牠也不睬我，
我也不踩牠，當然，我會很小心
翼翼小心；如果能飛，
我一定邀牠，一起高飛
一起遠走
我有很多地方，
還沒去過
譬如我夢中的一座高山，
那是聖山，我希望在那裡
不來也不去了！
如果我能真正去到那裡，
我是多麼希望，我的貓
也能永遠在一起
那是夢裡，也希望是夢外
我的貓，牠應該了解
更準確的說，我應該先了解牠
別讓牠怪我，我始終都是
重視牠，對牠
其實，我是沒有脾氣的
不能有脾氣！

（2017.07.18／16:38 胡思公館店）

As-a-Matter-of-Factly, I don't Have

The moon has it short temper. Who can't have hot or quick temper?

She's changed the first and fifteenth day of every month in the lunar calendar, I've got a bad nasty one.

My kitten, has also got one

We don't always play blind,

Sometimes loving to play blind

Playing a little bit but I don't care about it

Neither does it care for me

I don't care about it either, of course, I'll be very careful

With so meticulous a care that, if I could fly,

I'll surely invite it, to go flying together for

Going away high and wide together

I have many places to go, that

Haven't been to any yet;

For example, in my dream there's a high mountain,

That's a holy mountain, I hope to stay there never

Come in again and not go out again!

If I could really go there,

How much I've been hoping, my kitten

Can also be with me together forever

That's in the dream. As well as out of or beyond the dream

My kitten, that should realize

To be more exact, I should first understand it

Don't let it blame me,

I'm always paying great attention to it, from start to end

In fact, I've got no bad temper

I just can't afford to have any temper!

盛夏・剩下

后羿射下的九顆太陽，
千億年療傷之後，今夏已痊癒
——回到天上
天下萬物均已乾透，
剩下遍地
枯骨，齊將成灰⋯⋯

（2017.07.21／08:39 研究苑）

The Mid-summer at Its Highest Heat,
What's Left or Sheng-xia? Nothing!

Hou-yi, the legendary ancient hero general, falling in love with Chang-Err, the fair lady in the moon,
   used his arch to shoot down nine suns, on his own
After the healing process extended that and lasted for over hundred billion years, till this summer their
   healing treatment would have been done and the illness cured
One by one the suns all returned to the sky
All the beings in the world have been dried up thoroughly,
With only their dead bones left everywhere, all of which will be turned into ashes......

想，是用心的

總是半夜醒來，我在找我的貓
其實，現在已過清晨三時；
其實，我的貓
牠在我腦海中，只不知
牠躲在我左腦還是右腦？其實，
連我自己都不知道
我用左腦還是右腦，想牠
每一次醒來，我都膽戰心驚
深怕牠怪我，我怎麼可以獨自睡著
其實，睡或不睡
我都有想牠；其實，最自私的
應該還是牠，牠
只管自己眯著眼，永遠不會告訴你
我在想你
當貓，牠就有這種好處；
這是一種特權，
只有牠可以擁有，我可憐的我
只有想牠的份，想再多也還是——
想，是無可救藥的，是一輩子的
想，是得專心的，想；
想，其實是相互
折騰……

（2017.07.23／04:18 研究苑）

Thinking about Someone,
You've Got to Use Your Brain out of the True Heart

Always getting awake at midnight, I'm looking for my kitten.

In fact, now it's already over three o'clock in the morning;

In fact my kitten is,

In my brain and mind, just unknowing where

It hides in my left brain or the right one? In fact,

Even me I don't know myself

Whether I use the left brain or the right one, to think about it

Each time waking up, I'm so fearful that it might blame me, how come I could fall asleep alone

In fact, to sleep or not to sleep

I'm constantly thinking about it; in fact, the most selfish

Should be it, for it

Only mind itself winking its napping eyes, never telling you what's happening

I'm thinking about you

To be a kitten, it's got this kind of strength, good merit;

This is a privilege,

Only it's capable of having that right, not me the poor one

I can only think about it, thinking about it too much that ends up to——

Think only, it's incurable, it's for the whole life

Thinking about it, is whole-heartedly and stays focused, thinking;

Thinking about, in fact it's mutually

Torturing or troubling each other……

下一站，仍在我心中

下一站，在我心中仍是
丹麥的福恩島，或哥本哈根；
那兒都是我去過的，
最遠的國度，我去過了
是我念念不忘的人生的驛站，
還有英國的倫敦，
斯特拉福
莎士比亞的故鄉
我的貓，
牠說牠都陪我去過
我們一起見過了安徒生，
在福恩島的奧登塞，他的故鄉
沒錯。
就在那裡，我看到了
小巷中沒有穿衣服的
國王在試穿新衣，以及小河中的小紙船
以及安徒生媽媽洗衣服的小河口；
我的貓，牠說牠是很有耐心的
都在我心中陪伴我
很難想像吧，我的貓說
我們都不懂丹麥語，我們都是啞巴
你怎麼能找到安徒生，還有他的美人魚
坐在河口守護著哥本哈根……

下一站，人生的道路
還有一大段，
我的貓問我，夜還是黑得很漫長
我們會在哪兒？
我回答牠，我還是充滿信心
你可以繼續留在我心上，
我們可以在天亮之前，抵達
我心中最暗的亮點……

（2017.07.26／00:33 研究苑）

The Next Stop, Is Still in My Heart

The next stop, hidden in my heart is still

The Fu-en Island, Denmark, or Copenhagen;

All those places that, I've been to before,

The farthest country I've been to

They're the unforgettable life stations,

Also included are London, the United Kingdom

Stratford, hometown to Shakespeare

My kitten,

It says it already accompanied me to visit there

We've been together to have met with Hans Christian Anderson

At Oden on the Fu-en Island, his hometown

That's right.

It's over there, I've seen it

In the small alley the naked king unclothed

Who was trying on his new dress, and the paper folded ship floating on the little river flowing on

Along with the little river mouth in which Mother Anderson did the laundry for her son

My kitten, it says it's very patient

Always staying in my heart enjoying the company

It may be hard to imagine, my kitten said

We both don't understand the Norwegian language; we both are dumb-founded and deafened

How could you find Anderson, and his Mermaid?

Sitting at the mouth of the river watching over Copenhagen......

The next stop, the pathway of life

Then still there's a long journey deep and far to go ahead of us

My kitten asked me, the night is still darkened and lengthened, long and distant

Where would we be going or staying?

I replied to it; I'm still full of confidence

You may continue to stay on in my heart,

We may be able, before the dawn, to arrive at......

The darkest lightening point

貓，牠愛管我

昨天，我的貓和我吵了一架
正確的說，是昨天晚上
已過了零時零分，我還在寫詩
牠罵我：你怎麼可以愛你的詩
比愛我多多
愛我，比較少少
已是午夜了，牠說
你為什麼不快快躺下來，
可以在睡眠中，想我；
我能怎麼說呢？我沒有還嘴，
照說，是牠在嘮叨
我習慣只有聽牠的份，
其實
寫詩哪有你說要停就停？
詩，你要她來，她就來嗎
我知道，我的貓的習氣
牠喜歡佔有，最好是
24 小時，你都乖乖給牠
像牠一樣，眯著眼
但不一定要睡著；
我說我的貓，牠愛和我吵架
其實不是，是我的貓
牠愛管我，已經習慣……

（2017.07.27／15:27 捷運板南線，我要去胡思）

My Kitten, Loves Controlling Me

Yesterday, my kitten had a squabble with me arguing noisily with me

To be exact, it's yesterday night

Already passing zero hour and zero minute when I was still writing poems

It cursed me by saying: how can you love your poems so much

Much more than you love me

Loving me so far less than

It's midnight, it said

Why don't you lie down right away?

You can think about me in the dream, missing me;

What can I say to respond? I didn't talk back in reply,

True to say, that's her nagging

I'm accustomed to just listening to what it said

As a matter of fact

How come I stop writing poems at whims and, off and on, as you say?

Any poem, does she come out as you wish or please them to get to come

I know, the habit and nature of my kitten

It likes to domineer and control, you'd better obediently let it

Have the entire twenty-four hours of your time tamely

Like it, squinting its eyes

But not necessarily falling asleep;

I say my kitten; it loves squabbling with me

In fact, it's not so, as it's my kitten

It loves controlling and disciplining me; it's its habit to behave so......

妳就是我的貓

不敢想妳，也在想妳
我的貓，我們都在
三萬三千公尺的高空，
三小時又三十分鐘，我都睜開眼
妳在我心中，我們是一起飛翔
我們將到一個微笑的國度，
這是我熟悉的，
妳也不陌生，一年一會
十年又一年，因為小詩
因為有個磨坊；一天24小時，
天天24小時，詩就如磨穀子
一粒粒，粒粒皆辛苦
一字字，字字嘔心瀝血

妳看到了嗎？妳躲在我心中，
妳一定看得很清楚，我就這麼著
這麼著，就年年春夏秋冬

春夏秋冬，就這麼著
這麼著，就是一輩子了
無怨無悔，我的貓
妳就是我的貓……

（2017.07.29／16:35 CI835 ／27F 台北飛曼谷途中，即將降低飛行）

You're My Kitten

Not daring to think about you, yet I can't resist three or stop thinking about you

My kitten, we're now both

At the height of thirty thousand and three thousand meters dhigh up in the sky,

During the flight of three hours and thirty minutes long, I keep opening my eyes wide

You're in my mind, as we're soaring and flying together

We're going to visit a smiling country, to me.

That's a familiar place

It's also not strange for you to attend a meeting once a year

Ten years plus one year, because of the mini poems

Because there's a mill to grind, working twenty-four hours clock a day,

Day in day out around the clock, the poems are just like grinding grains and wheat

Grain by grain, every grain of it takes efforts and gets painful to be ground into powder

Word by word, each word must take infinite pain working my heart out to write them into a poem

Do you see that? You hide deep in my innermost heart,

You must see it very carefully, as I'm working this hard

Working this way, year in year out, in all seasons; spring, summer, autumn, and winter

Spring, summer autumn and winter, that's the way I'm doing the milling

All through this way, that's a whole life as my work career

Without any complaints and any regrets, my kitten

You're my kitten......

(2017.07.29 / 16:35CI835 / 27F on flight to Bangkok in low flying attitude)

夜會朝太陽方向

早安。太陽在東方，
我還在微笑的國度，佛祖保佑
今天，我將移動
朝太陽方向，
去一個全新的地方
我重新出發，從心出發
我的貓會一起同行，
牠只要在我心上，或睡或眯眼
不會吵我
我搭車，我顛簸
或乘飛機，或穿越雲端
牠都不用操心，
我能為牠著想，照顧好自己
有一種愛，叫放心
無論走多遠，我的貓
都會留在我心上
守著我；我剛剛路過，
右邊是海，是黑黑的，有沙灘
我在芭堤雅海邊，
夜晚是美好的，一切雜亂
——不見
舞台亮麗，聲光燦爛
是歌舞，是歡樂，穿越時空
有變性美女，嘆為觀止……

（2017.07.31／23:32 芭堤雅LONG BEACH GARDEN Hotel）

The Night Will Face the Sunshine

Good morning. The sun's rising in the east,

I'm still in the kingdom of smiles, blessed by Buddha

Today, I'll be moving towards the direction of where

The sun is facing,

Heading to a totally brand-new place

I'll restart, starting refreshing, from the bottom of my heart

My kitten will be traveling with me together,

It'll only be staying in my heart, sleeping or blinking or winking

Won't bothering or annoying me

I take the vehicle, and I jolt on a bumpy road

Or take an airplane, or pierce through the clouds

My kitten doesn't have to be concerned or worried,

I'm able to think about it, hoping it can take care of itself

There's a kind of love, whose name is to let go off

And rest assured to be at ease worry-free

No matter how far I go, my kitten

Is always in my heart

Watching over me; I've just passed by along the way,

On the right side it's the sea, all dead dark and black, with sand beach

I'm at the Bataya sea beach,

The night is beautiful, everything messy is out t of sight and

Disappearing one by one

The stage is brilliant and splendid, with the sound and light being shining and resplendent

There are songs and dances, full of joy and happiness, that is piercing through time and space

There are trans-sexual beauties, wow! it takes my breath away as nothing can be better than this exotic
  performance of perfection

在芭堤雅海灘

早安。六點。我在芭堤雅海邊，
我的貓陪我，牠在我心上
靜靜坐著
陪我，讀沙灘
讀風，讀風吹過的旗語，讀浪花
又讀時間，
讀狗狗走過的腳印，
讀剛剛消逝的時間，
讀剛剛湧上又退下的浪濤，
讀自己的心事，讀一波波浪花
讀無人陪伴的時間，讀時間的孤單和孤獨
讀時間的無聊和時間的虛空，
讀時間的無所事事和讀沙灘上的一隻拖鞋
和一張空椅子，又讀一座海的心事
和一粒粒的細沙，在芭堤雅的海邊……

（2017.08.02／07:12 泰國芭堤雅海邊）

At the Beach of Bataya, Thailand

Good morning! It's Six O'clock. I'm at the Bataya Beach,

My kitten's accompanying me, who's is in my mind

Sitting quietly

Spending time with me, gazing at the sandy beach like reading it

Reading the wind, reading the words of flags fluttering blown in the wind, reading the white top surging waves

Also reading time,

Reading the footprints left by the dogs that were walking by,

Reading the time just passing and passed

Reading the just surging waves raging up and then receding and sunk,

Reading the inner secrets deep in the heart, reading the flower-like waves one by one

Reading the time being alone without the company, reading the lonely time be alone in solicitude

Reading the boredom of time and emptiness of time

Reading time of doing nothing else and reading a slipper left on the sandy beach

As well as an empty chair, also reading a huge sea forits stories and secrets in the heart

And a grain of fine sand, at the Bataya Beach......

欠債的，要還

今天是父親節，我的貓
一大早就在我心裡，
祝賀我
父親節快樂，
我非常感動
流了好多熱淚，可以裝滿一瓶
高粱酒的空酒瓶
可惜，我的貓
牠不一定能看得到，牠只活在
我心裡，如果我的淚是可以倒流的，
牠或許就能看得清楚，我為什麼
要流那麼多高興的熱淚？
其實，也不是高興
而是悲傷和歉疚；因為，
我爸爸在的時候，我都不懂得
該如何在這一天，表達我對他
感恩的心意！現在，我懂了
活在世間，人人都是欠債的
你懂得如何還嗎？
你還過父母的什麼？
也不只是父母，或妻子丈夫兒女
也不只是兄弟姊妹，還有師長貴人，
也不只是認識的，還有不認識的
我們都還過了嗎？還有
我們曬過的陽光，
我們吹過的風，
我們呼吸過的空氣，
我們淋過的雨，
我們喝過的水，甚至是
我們生存的環境，
大自然的一草一木，等等……

欠債的，要還
你還過了嗎？
你還夠了嗎？
我的貓和我，
四目對望
仰天，呼喚
一致茫然！

（2017.08.08／12:33 研究苑）

Be Sure to Repay the Debt Due!

Today's Father's Day, my kitten

Very early in the morning is persent in my heart,

To celebrate me on the occasion

Saying to me Happy Father's Day,

That makes very much touched and moved

Into causing my tears to be welling up in my eyes streaming down the cheeks that can fill the whole
   bottle capacity of

An empty Gao-liang Wine bottle

Unfortunately, my kitten

Is necessarily able to see me, as it only lives

In my heart, provided my tears could go reversely and be flown back,

It would be able to see more clearly, why I'm shedding

So many bitter tears out of joy and happiness?

In fact, it's not out of happiness

But out of sadness and regrets; because,

When my dad was living with me, I even didn't know

How and what I should do to express my gratitude to him on this day! Now, I got it

For expressing my gratefulness from the bottom of my heart!

Living in this world, everyone is to repay some debts due, you know how to repay it?

Did you repay your parents anything?

Not just your parents, or your wife or husband and children

Not just your siblings, also your teachers and those someone right there who do you a favor lifting you
   up, helping you get ahead,

Not just those whom you know, also those who you don't

Have we all repaid them already? Also the sunshine that gives us warmth and tan,

The winds that have blown us on,

The air we've been breathing,

The rains that are falling upon us,

The waters we've drunk, even the environment in which we are living

Any all the grass and trees in great nature,

What's been owed by us, we must pay back duly

Have you repaid yet?

Enough of it?

My kitten with me

Face to face, eyeball to eyeball

Looking up at the sky, calling and shouting

But feeling in a boundless puzzlement and blankness.

仲夏，家具們開會.1

今天，主人不在家
大人小孩都不在家；
我的貓，牠有想法
召集家具們開會——
首先，牠說
我們需要有一個當主席，
所有家具都舉手：
我要，我要，我也要……
我的貓說，那就
用民主的方式選舉，
與會的代表個個都有資格，
現在我們就開始投票：
高個子的酒吧椅，站起來，一票。
寂寞的長條木板椅，躺著，一票。
愛睏的搖搖椅，搖一搖，一票。
愛抱抱的沙發，坐著，一票。
胖胖的大圓桌，自己摸摸圓肚子，也一票。
什麼都不想的小板凳，最矮，也一票……
我的貓，跳上最高的酒吧椅
牠宣布說：
以民主的方式選舉結果，
現在你們每一位都有一票，
最後我想想，還是由我當主席
你們大家都聽我的，首先
把冷氣關掉，
天氣太熱了，我們國家的電力
不夠，大家都乖乖留在原位
和我一起，睡午覺！

（2017.08.10／14:45 高鐵嘉義北上車將到板橋）

The Furniture Family's Midsummer Meeting No.1

Today, Master's out; he's not home

All the adults and children are not home;

My kitten, who's got an idea

That's to call all the pieces of furniture to meet—

First of, it gets started, saying

We'd need someone to act as Chairperson,

All the pieces of furniture are raising their hands to say aye;

I want to be, I want, choose me, me, too......

My kitten says, then let's

Hold first an election in a democratic way,

All the participants present are qualified to chair,

Now start to cast the votes:

The tall fellow bar chair, stands up, one vote.

The lonely long wooden bench, lying on its back, one vote.

The always sleepy or napping armchair, shaking and wavering, one vote.

The sofa loving hugging, seated, one vote.

The fat huge round-table, feeling its own round ball-like belly, one vote.

The little stool reluctant to think of anything big, the shortest, also cast a vote......

My kitten, jumping onto the tallest bar chair,

Making the announcement:

The result of the democratic election,

Is that now each of you got a vote,

At last, I'm thinking, it's proper and good for me to serve as Chairperson

All of you must follow and listen to me, first,

Turn off the air conditioner,

It's too hot, the capacity of electric power in our country

Is not sufficient, everybody must stay where you belong, together with me, taking a nap!

早安。午安。晚安

早安。午安。晚安。
日安。夜安。
日日安。月月安。年年安……
凡我生命中的人，我都時時
在我心裡，向他們問安
祝福

人生苦短，這趟旅程
有時覺得，是滿漫長
我常常自己一個人走，
自己習慣自己
一個人，自己走；
有很長一段時間，我沒有和我的貓
在心底裡對話，
我的貓
牠一定會以為我有問題，甚至誤解
我不再理牠；
甚至以為，我已
不在人這個世界了！

我的貓，是很單純的，
其實，我和我的貓一樣
單純，只不知我該如何對牠
如何怎麼說？
人生，難免有許多種種
無奈低落，
不知所以
我能怎麼說，就最好不說；
再天大的事，想想它就過了！
還有什麼好說，可以說？

我的貓，請別誤會
我和妳一樣，常常喜歡自己
自己，靜靜的
想

（2017.08.11／15:24 捷運昆陽站要去胡思）

Good Morning, Good afternoon, Good Evening

Good morning. Good afternoon. Good evening.

Good day. Good night.

Be good every day. Be good every month, be good every year……

Anyone entering my life, who is always in my heart, I wish them

All the best

Life is too short, in this life journey

Sometimes it feels, so long long-drawned and prolonged a period of time

Often I walk alone, along the way

One lonely person, walk on my own by myself;

For a very long period of time, I've not dialogued heart to heart.

With my kitten

My kitten,

It must think that I've got some problem, even with misunderstanding

I no longer care about it;

I even think, I haven't been

Living in this human world!

My kitten, it's very simple-minded,

In fact, me and my kitten are both

Simple and pure, just wondering how I should treat it?

And how to talk to it?

In life, there's inevitably a lot of things

Helpless that makes us feel low-spirited and despirited.

Just don't know why

How can I say it? it's better not say or pour it out;

No matter how big a matter, just give it a quick thought, it's gone then and passing away.

What else can I say? What may I say?

My kitten, please don't wrong me

Me and you, both always like

Ourselves, quietly pondering

Thinking

仲夏，家具們開會.2

天氣太熱了！今天還是要開會；
主要議題是
我們該不該限電？我的貓說，
我的終極目標是
要建立一個非核家園。
現在開始，踴躍發言。

無聊的會議桌打哈欠說，我想睡覺。
寂寞的餐桌違心的說，我想開冷氣。
發呆的椅子不知好歹的說，你們最好不要煩我。
想出走的沙發欠揍的說，我最討厭有人想賴著不走。
愛做夢的蓆夢思眯著眼說，我很想忘掉一切。
常常抱怨的長板凳說，誰要涼快就早點躺下來。
不搖不行的搖搖椅說，熱得天昏地暗了還開什麼會！

以上發言都十分珍貴，我把它們記下來
一一都列入提案；我的貓總結說，
你們的發言我都很重視，我會一一
列為我的施政的重要參考。今天，
很好，我們就到此為止

天氣實在是太熱了，我們都不需要加油，
大家沒事，就繼續睡午覺吧
祝福！

（2017.08.12／15:39 研究苑／次日09:44 修訂）

The Furniture Family's Midsummer Meeting No. 2

It's way too hot! Today we still need to hold this meeting;

The main theme or issue is

On whether we should effect limited use of electric power, my kitten says,

My ultimate goal is

To build a nuclear power-free home.

Now go ahead, please give your opinions and thoughts freely and openly as you can

The bored conference table said, yawning, I wanna feel like going to sleep.

The lonely dining table uttered his words against its will and conscience, saying, I hope to turn on the air-conditioner.

The chair in a trance playing fool said not knowing good from bad, chalk from cheese, you all better not bother me.

Wanting to go out, the sofa said improperly indiscreet, lacking the tact not knowing how far it could go, I hate most those who continued to stay in here hanging on, lingering around.

The dream-loving Simmons spring bed winking its eyes, said, I intend very much to forget about all these.

Always complaining, the long bench stool said, who want to feel cool, lies down immediately.

Keeping swinging and shaking, the armchair said, it's already terribly hot like a murky sky on the dark earth, what the devil for holding this god-damned meeting!

All you've said above are very valuable and pertinent, I've already recorded them all.

一one by one I listed them in our proposal; my kitten concluded,

I've paid special attention to what you said and expressed, so I'm going to

List them as important referenced agenda.Today,

Very good, let's call it a day. The meeting is dismissed.

It's indeed too burning hot a day, we all need not cheer up at work,

If there's nothing else to raise or move, go on taking your nap.

God bless you!

療時間之殤

咖啡療傷。我自己說的，
我將從機會主義者，升級
每天一杯；
因有好友送的
一套精美磨豆機，
我得學會自己磨，自己沖泡
療時間之殤！
我的貓，是貼心的
牠說，要是你喝了不能睡呢？
我說，
那正好想她……
反正今天的時間，明天的時間
時間過了還有時間，
我已經不太會管理時間，
頂多不睡的時候，就寫詩
或想什麼的什麼，也可以
我的貓，牠應該知道的
其實不用問我，更不必為我操心
濾紙濾過的時間，之後的時間
還能剩下多少，那是
苦苦的一杯，我最是喜歡的
就是這樣
美式的一種，黑咖啡。

（2017.08.14／22:33 研究苑）

A Healing Time to Stop Dying Young Immaturely

Coffee can heal wounds. That's my own opinion and thoughts.,

I'll lift my status up to more from a casual coffee drinker or any opportunist into an a-mug-of-coffee-a-day
  consumer.

Because a good friend of mine gifted me

A whole set of refined coffee bean grinder,

I have to learn to grind coffee beans myself, make coffee on my own to heal the wound of time!

My kitten, so very considerate and thoughtful

It says, what'd happen if you couldn't sleep after drinking coffee?

I say,

That's great I could be thinking about it my dear kitten......

Anyway today I've got today's time, tomorrow I've got another new day of time.

Time passed, and then there comes new time again,

I've not cared about time management too hard,

At most, when I'm not sleeping or sleepless, I can write poems

Or thinking what's about what, or maybe

My kitten who should know

In fact, no need to ask me for the advice, let alone to worry me.

The time being screened through a screen paper, afterward it turns out to be time

How much of time still left, that's

A cup of bitter coffee, I like most such a bitter one

American style, black coffee.

心事只寫那一行

心事只寫兩行，但何止兩行
如果只寫一行，該寫什麼？
我的貓說，就寫
你想我；
牠習慣躲在我心裡，我們的對話
常常這樣開始，也常常
這樣結束，我們都不在乎
要在乎什麼？只要牠仍習慣
躲在我心中，
是安全的；不論我去到哪裡，
再遠也不過仍在這個地球，
或許也有可能，那是有一天──
那一天，終會到來
我們都有信心，也不害怕
我們仍然同時在一起，
不是消失
對話，就是你和我
我的貓說，心事還是
只寫那一行；一行
一行就夠了！

（2017.08.15／15:37 捷運板南西門將轉新店去公館胡思）

One Liner on Heart Secret Stories

Only two lines written on heart secret stories, but it requires more than two, instead.

But if only one line is allowed, what should one write about?

My kitten says, simply writes:

You miss me;

It used to hide in my heart, our dialog

Often so it begins, so does it end; we don't care about that at all

What should we care about? As long as it's still used to be

Hidden in my heart,

It's safe, no matter where I go,

No matter how far it is, it's still within this globe,

Maybe it's possible, that's some day—

That day, will finally come

We both are confident, nor are we afraid of it

We still are together at the same time,

Not disappearing or vanishing

A dialogue. That's between you and me

My kitten said, the stories on heart secret can still be told

Only in that one single line; one liner

One line is enough!

我搶時間

時間，不是我的
我沒有時間，我搶時間
已成為慣犯。我的貓
警告我，
我會受到最嚴厲的懲罰，
這是天大的竊盜之罪！
明白，長久以來
我明知故犯，
習性難改；我願我以我終身
寫詩贖罪，
我向我的貓，誠懇保證
每天一首，最好天天都有
以詩心代替坐牢
我的貓說，你能自知理虧
牠也願意坐在我心牢，
陪伴我，一年兩年
直到永遠，永遠……

（2017.08.17／21:47 研究苑）

Grab the Time
—Carpe Diem

Time, it's not mine

I don't have much left; I must hurry scrambling to race or fight against the clock to grab the time as fast
 as I can

Having been a habitual time robber. My kitten once

Warned me,

I might get the hardest punishment,

It's the greatest crime for stealing that I've committed!

Having understood, since a long time ago

I've known that, but, still committed it again on purpose

I can't break it, correcting my wrong habit; so I'll repent for my sin by writing poems the whole life,

I sincerely assure my kitten of this

One poem a day, better write them every day by using my heart, brain and mind of poetry to study

My kitten says, you're able to know you're wrong

It's also willing to be imprisoned in the heart cage in place of me,

Staying with me, one year or two

Till forever and, eternally for good......

晚安，一起去散步

我們一起去散步。很久沒有聽到這聲音，
這聲音來自我自己的心裡，特別熟悉
我的貓就是我聽到的這個聲音的發源處，
非常明確；
沒有別的可以假借，這世界上
再也沒有什麼需要告白；我只是我的
內心或外在的代言，如此可以信任
我就是那個百分之百的九十九點幾之一，
轉變了我們的現代之實；

有很長一段日夜，我們是失聯的
日和月；我們彼此都不曾抱怨，
該不該嘆息，就讓它們自我完成
自己的寂寞和孤獨
虹要是能從那個山頭升起，我們也可以
明理讓路，等時間再度降臨
給予足夠的空間，我們仍然攜手歡迎

我們一起去散步！ 我聽到
是久違的聲音，穿越自己心中的
千萬座山谷和丘陵
它是熟悉的……

（2017.08.24／22:20 研究苑）

Good Evening, Let's Go for a Walk

We go take a walk together. For a long time, I've not heard this inner voice,

That comes from my heart, sounding especially familiar

My kitten is the source of the voice I've heard

Very clearly and definitely;

There's nothing else to be borrowed or replaced, in this world

There's nothing else I need to express or state; I'm only

Such a spokesperson internally or outside on my own, in such a trustworthy way

Me, I'm that one point of mine hundred ninety-ninth out of 100%,

That can be transformed into our modern reality;

For a very long period of time, day in and day out, we have lost contact with or connection to each other

Over days and months; we've not complained at each other,

Whether we should sigh or not, just let them go self-fulfilling

Their own loneliness and being in solitude

Provided the rainbow could rise from the mountain summit, we might have made way to yield

Reasonably and understandably, waiting for the time to arrive again

Able to provide sufficient space, so that we still can greet and welcome hand in hand

We take a walk together! What I've heard is that long missing voice inside, piercing through and into my
  heart where

They are those ten million mountains and hilly high lands

They are so familiar.......

唇，它有很重要的工作

情人節，快樂！
天下的人，都是情人，情人節
大家快樂。
一杯咖啡，我每天都喝它，
但今天不同；
我會想
它該幾度，幾度才好喝？
我喜歡熱，燙更好
但我會小心，我知道
我跟我的貓說
愛要懂得呵護，
珍惜我們每個人的
每一天
每一天，都是情人節；我非爛情，
我只想
這世界有太多缺憾，太多無情的事故
不斷發生，我們該如何彌補？

我的貓已走進我的夜裡，牠不再聽我
　嘮叨
夜裡，有很多安靜
很多夢想，包括夢想不到的
都要認領，要認養
要用夢來養，養它更多的小夢
夜裡的星星，我們都要抬頭仰望
包括它們的夢，也包括螢火蟲
和螢火蟲的夢；我是這樣想，
我也這樣認為我有的，它們都要有
我沒有的，它們都該有
情人節快樂，不只一天
也不只一杯咖啡，
燙的，不讓它傷到心
也別讓它傷到唇，
唇，還有很重要的工作
要它全心全意的負責

（2017.08.28／七夕早晨.研究苑）

A Very Important Task for Lips to Do

Double Seventh Valentine's Day based on Chinese lunar calendar, be happy on Chinese Lovers' festival!

All the people on earth, are lovers, on Lovers' Day

A Happy Day to all.

A cup of coffee I drink it every day, but today it's different;

I would think

What degree of the warmth for the temperature, is best or ideal for the heat temperature of the drink

I like it hot, the more boiling one is the better

But I'll be careful, I know that

I told my kitten that

To love is to know how to care for or about your lover,

Treasuring and cherishing everyone's

life on a daily basis

Each and every day, is Valentine's Day; I'm very much passionate for falling in love

I'm just pondering

In this world there are too many things of regrets, defects and imperfections as there are too many relentless and merciless events coming up and going on

Keeping on happening, what should we do to make up or even perfect them?

My kitten has already got into my night; it won't listen to me any more of

My nagging

In the night, there's much quietness and serenity

There are a lot of dreams, including what can't be dreamed about

That I must take them and adopt and raise them

Using the dreams to keep and breed them, so as to raise more small dreams

To gaze at the stars in the night, we all need to raise our heads to look them up there

Including the dreams, also about fire-worms

And the dreams made by fire fireworms; I'm so thinking,

I also think so that as long as I have what I've had, they should also have what I have.

Even what I haven't had, they should all have.

Happy Double Seventh Valentine's Day, not just for one day, neither just for a cup of coffee,

It's boiling hot not allowing it to burn or hurt the heart

Not letting it hurt your lips,

Lips, are still playing a very important role in this day.

It's been asked to wholeheartedly hold accountable for them.

種子，閉著眼睛

閉著眼睛，你能看到什麼？
我的貓常常問我，我也常常問我自己
因此，我就開始學習
睡覺時，我能看到什麼？
做夢吧！有一個聲音，
它很清楚的告訴我，我沒有睜開眼睛；
那聲音不是熟悉的，我可以肯定
它絕對不是我的貓發出的聲音
我繼續尋找，在我的夢裡
尋找那聲音來自的地方，我可以肯定
我還在夢裡，我是閉著眼睛
我也可以說，我是睡著的
我看到了，我看到了我自己
小小的自己，還在母親的子宮裡
我仰望的天空，我瞭望的海洋
它們都讓我放心成長；

從母親的子宮裡，如即將破殼的
一粒種子
我張開了兩片嫩芽，我看到了
東方，有一顆小小的
小太陽……

（2017.08.30／17:27 胡思公館店）

Seedlings, with Their Eyes Closed

Closing your eyes, and what can you see?

My kitten always asks me, and I often ask me the same question.

Therefore, I begin to learn

While sleeping, what can I see?

Pursue and make a dream! There's an innermost voice,

It's clearly telling me. I haven't opened my eyes wide yet;

That's not a familiar voice. I'm sure or positive

It absolutely not from my kitten

I go on searching, in my dream

Seeking for the original source of that voice, so I can be sure

I'm still in my dream, I'm keeping my eyes closed

Or I may as well say, I'm sleeping

I saw it, as I saw myself

A small insignificant me, which is still staying in my Mom's womb

I looked up at the sky, and I look afar at the ocean

They all let me grow carefree at ease;

From the womb of my mom, me just like a seedling

Going to break through the shell

I opened two half pieces of the green budding, just to have seen and noticed

In the east, there's a small, tiny version of the....

我永遠陪著你

我說我迷路了！在自己心裡，
偷偷摸摸，黑黑暗暗
走不出去；我的貓說
就不要出去，
天下不是很亂嗎？
在心裡，有我陪你
我們就一直在一起，
我也不用想你，我就知道
你在哪裡，那裡也是
在我心裡
我說我迷路了！不只是現實的，
還有精神的迷路，我走不出去；
孔子教我的，三省吾身
我只省一省，都醒不過來
柏拉圖告訴我的，那
理想國怎麼走？
我是真的迷惑了，
困在自己的心中！
我的貓，是一隻靈貓
但牠現在只能告訴我，
你別煩惱，我就會永遠陪著你
我們繼續探索……

（2017.09.01／17:02 研究苑）

I'll be With You for Good

I say I get lost losing my way! In my mind,

Stealthily sneaking around, in the dead darkness

I can't go out; my kitten said

You'd better not go out,

Will there not be in the hubbub of the chaotic life of the world?

In the mind, there's me being around with you

Then we've been together all the time,

I don't need to think about you either; I'll know that

Wherever you are, that's also where my mind or heart is located

I say I get lost! Not just in the reality world

There's a kind of getting lost spiritually or mentally, that I can't get out of it;

Just as Confucius taught me, we should reflect and examine on ourselves for at least three times or three
  things on what we have been doing everyday

I only take one round of refection or two, then I can't wake up from it

As Plato told me, then

Where should we head to go to the Republic?

I'm actually puzzled and confused,

Entangled like being imprisoned in my own heart!

My kitten, it's a cat of spirituality

But now it can only tell me,

You don't worry, then I'll be around with you forever

We'll continue to explore and search.....

今夜，我在想牠

常常我在最深最黑的
夜裡，回到我心裡
去看看我的貓是否還在
我心裡？常常是
已經超過一個禮拜了，
今夜我才安然真正的回到了我心裡，
在夠深夠黑夠暗的夜裡，我沒有吵醒牠
牠仍然睡得好好，我才放心
我說常常想，一日不知幾回
幾回才會真正回到自己的心裡，
而安安靜靜的
聽自己的心聲，聽我的貓的甜甜的
鼾聲？打呼的恬恬，靜靜
今夜，我是在想牠了
是常常之後久久之後再回頭，
長長久久，常常
在想牠……

（2017.09.11／19:22 研究苑／剛回到山區的家）

Tonight, I'm Thinking about It
—the Kitten

At times I'm in the deepest and darkest,

Dead night, whence I return to my heart once again

To see if my kitten is still in there

In my heart? Always it is

Already more than one week that has elapsed

Tonight I'm safely coming back in peace to my heart,

In the night that's deep and dark enough, I don't bother to disturb it to not wake it up

It still sleeps soundly, and hence I can feel at ease, relieved and relaxed

I'm always pondering, how many times a day I am really returning to my heart,

So peacefully and quietly

Hearing my heart talking, and hearing my kitten giving off its sweet

Snoring? That's so peaceful and serene a thing to have,

Tonight, I'm thinking about it

It often comes back again after a long, long period of time,

Long, long time, as I'm always

Thinking about it......

什麼什麼無關

什麼什麼無關，什麼什麼跟什麼有關
什麼跟什麼無關？
我這樣想的時候，無非是想和自己的腦子
做一些練習，我的貓
牠就半夜醒來罵我，無聊透頂
為什麼睡得好好的，
為什麼
要半夜醒來想無用的課題，
寫無用的詩？
眉毛跟眼睛有什麼關係？
鼻子跟耳朵有什麼關係？
嘴巴跟嘴唇有什麼關係？
這些什麼跟什麼都沒有了
有什麼關係？
我這樣反覆思考的時候，我知道我
寫詩跟這些根本都沒有關係，也都有
關係；
它們都裝在我的臉上，跟我不能沒有的
就有關係，我就找到了它們的新關係.
誰也不能沒有這些
眼、鼻、耳、嘴，再加上可有可無的
裝飾性很強的眉毛，在眼睛之上
想要飛起來的，一扇一扇
一上，一上
卻又永遠也飛不起來的，那又有什麼
關係？
什麼什麼跟什麼什麼和什麼什麼跟什麼，
都沒有關係！

（2017.09.12／03:21 研究苑）

What's Nothing to Do with Anything Else Is Something that Has Nothing else to Do

What's not to do with anything. What's anything to do with something else?

What's nothing to do with else?

While I'm thinking this way, it's because I'm thinking of providing in my brain

With some practice and exercises, yet involving my kitten

It would get awoken at midnight to curse or abuse me, that's an extremely boring thing to death

Why during my sound sleep?

Why does it wake up at midnight to bother me with the use of such useless topics or issues,

To want to write useless poems?

Is there anything to do with eyebrows in relationship with eyes?

What's the relationship between a nose and the ears?

What's that of the mouth in relationship with lips?

What do these that have nothing to do has anything to do with it?

Like pondering on this I'm repetitively pondering, I realize I

When writing my poems that has nothing to do with all these anyway;

They're installed and equipped on my face, along with what I can't be missing out in such

Relationships, so that I can get the new relationship.

Nobody can afford to miss these

Eyes, noses, ears, mouths, plus those optional items

For the highly decorative eye-brows that are located above the eyes

Which are desiring to fly, one by one

One going up following another up

Yet they can't fly up forever, does it matter if there's not any relationship?

What's what with anything to do with what's nothing to do with what,

There's nothing to do at all!

101 忠狗的心聲

我用專注的眼神，正在看你
你以為我是流浪的狗嗎？
正是。我的主人，
始亂終棄！我沒有怨她，
我在巷口，徘徊幾天
包括日和夜；你知道吧！
狗是忠於主人的。
我說我已徘徊幾天，
我沒有吃的，
我不願像其他流落在城裡的狗，
我不去扒任何一個垃圾筒；
我是有原則的，我有我的尊嚴
我是101 忠狗的後裔，
我不是什麼阿貓阿狗，我就是
101 忠狗！

（2017.09.13／16:14 在270 公車上）

The Heart Talk of the 101 Dalmatians

With my focused look, I'm watching over you

You thought of me as a dog going astray?

Exactly. My master,

You abandoned me after having played up with! I haven't hated that master.

I'm at the entrance of the alley, lingering for several days

Throughout day and night; you know that!

Dogs are faithful and loyal to their masters.

I said I'd been lingering for several days,

I have nothing to eat,

I am not like other astray dogs getting lost downtown in the city,

I won't rake and gather up garbage in any trash can;

I'm a principled dog, and I've kept my own dignity

Being the descendant of a faithful Dalmatian,

I'm no ordinary cat or dog, I'm

One of the 101 Dalmatians

心情十行

我的心情，是有顏色的
閉著眼睛，我在冥思；
我的頭髮，也有心情；
黑的，有輕度憂傷；
藍的，有海洋不確定的
風浪；那些起伏的悲歡
該屬於檸檬的顏色，
最多的紅，就讓它持續燃燒
明日，明日的旅程
不必在乎，我選擇繼續漂流……

（2017.09.19／19:59 研究苑）

Ten Liners on Feelings and Moods

In my mood, it is colorful

With my eyes closed, I'm meditating;

My hair, has got its mood;

The black one, is slightly sad;

The blue one, has got the uncertainty of the ocean

In the wind the rolling and soaring waves; reflecting those vicissitudes of ups and downs of sadness and
　happiness in life

which should belong to lemon color

The greatest are red in color, and then let them keep firing scorching and burning

Tomorrow, the journey for tomorrow

Don't care a bit about it, I chose to go on wandering and floating......

袋鼠不是每隻都有袋子

袋鼠不是每隻都有袋子，
牠們站起來，被我看到了
前面兩隻腳，都瘦瘦小小
以為都患了小兒麻痺症，
走路四肢落地，一定很辛苦！
是的，很辛苦，
就因為這樣
牠們就不喜歡走路，
習慣用跳的，
跳的比走的快
快又方便
袋鼠有袋，不
只有袋鼠媽媽才有袋子，
那叫
育嬰袋。小袋鼠不會跳的時候，
媽媽就用這個袋子保護牠，
敵人來了就可以逃得快！
跳跳跳，袋鼠媽媽就是這樣
這麼可愛
牠愛牠自己，也愛牠的寶寶

（2017.09.27／10:01 在澳洲墨爾本In Melbourne, Australia）

Not Every Kangaroo Carries Its Belly Bag

Not every kangaroo has got a bag,

They stand up, and as it's seen by me

Their two front legs, both thin and small

Like having polis disease

Walking around with their four feet on, must be very painstaking

Yes, very difficult

They don't like walking,

And are accustomed to leaping,

Instead, they're jumping faster than walking

It's quicker swifter and easier

Kangaroo has a bag, not only

Mother kangaroo has got such a bag; it's called baby-nursing bag

When little kangaroos can't jump,

Mummy uses this bag to protect her baby,

When there's enemy they can escape and flee ever more quickly!

Jump and leap, leap and jump mother kangaroos are

So lovely

It loves itself, and loves her babies too.

玉山的野薔薇

野，非一般
野，是原生的純潔；
白，我的最愛
白，我一生堅持；
四片花瓣，綻放美笑
幸福的符碼；

你，看到了嗎？
喜歡，喜歡就送給你；
但請記住，
年年金夏，六七月
你一定要記住，請你
到我故鄉來；

我的故鄉，福爾摩沙
請你一定要登上
台灣的第一高峰──
玉山；是聖山，
全世界都知道，
亙古不變
白玉之山！

（2017.09.09／09:29 研究苑）

Yu Shan Wild Roses in Mt. Morrison:
the Jade Mountain

It's wild, but not ordinarily wild;

Being wild, it's in its originally and natively pure;

White color, it's my most favorite one

Whiteness, as my lifelong persistent loving the color;

The four pedaled flower, sprouting out a beautifully blooming smile

it's a lucky code;

Hey, you, do you notice that?

Like it, you like it, and let me pluck it down for you;

But please remember,

Every year in golden summer, in June and July

You've got to bear in mind, please you

Come visit my native hometown;

My hometown, Formosa

Please make sure to reach and land the highest mountain there on Taiwan

Yu-shan or Jade Mountain; it's the holy mountain;

Well-known by the whole world,

Constantly unchanged for ages and generations

From ancient to present

The world-famous mountain of pure white jade!

企鵝回巢

神仙小企鵝，個子最嬌小
最可愛；
走路喜歡抬頭，
東張西望
左肩右肩，搖搖晃晃
牠們最重視安全，
走路東張西望，
才不會被雜草絆倒。
神仙小企鵝，天黑了
才要回巢；
牠們從白花花的浪裡
跳上沙灘，都會先停下來
想想看
家是在城裡還是在郊區？
也同時等等同伴，
三五成群，結伴回家
感覺比較安全。
今晚，有好多人守在看台上
脖子都拉得很長，第一次要看
神仙小企鵝回巢，大家都很安靜
包括站在沙灘上，要迎接牠們的一群海鷗，連翅膀也緊緊收起來
不想驚嚇牠們。

神仙小企鵝，泡在大海裡一整天
牠們都很盡責，每隻公企鵝都會帶回
飽飽的鮮美魚蝦，
在胃裡
反芻咀嚼，要餵牠的母企鵝
和牠們的小企鵝⋯⋯

（2017,10.04／中秋 研究苑）

Home-coming Penguins

The little fairy penguins, as small fellows with its tiniest build are the cutest and
The loveliest;
When walking along, they like to raise their heads,
Looking around from east and west, back and forth
Swinging from its left shoulder and then to its right, swaggering and wavering hard
They pay the greatest attention to the safety issues,
A-walking, looking around to the east and then to the west,
So as not to tip falling by the weeds.
The fairy little penguins, not until it gets dark
They won't go back to their home nests;
Seeing from the white top waves
They'll first stop and ponder
Before jumping onto the sand beach,
Are their homes in the suburb or downtown?
They're also always waiting for their partners,
Three's and five's in group, heading home in groups together.
To feel surely safer.
Tonight, there are many people keeping staying on the platform,
Lengthening their necks longing to see for the first time
The fairy penguins going home nests, and they all keep quiet
Including a flock of seagulls standing on the sand beach, holding their wings tight, ready to greet them,
Not wanting to frighten or scare them away.

All the whole day long, the fairy penguins, soaked in the huge sea
They're all dutiful, each male penguin will take home
The tasty fresh fish and shrimps,
With fully packed stomachs,
Where they are repetitively chewed and digested to feed their female penguins in their stomachs
Before feed-backing them for their baby penguins......

一面窗之外

一面窗，我從內往外看
其實我應該由外往內看，
說得更白一點，我應該
看看自己的內心；
外面的人來人往，與我何干？
我該想想誰，而不該只看
人來人往
有風有雨，雨若打在我臉上
別誤以為我在流淚，傷心的往事
何其多，還有未來的風雨
作為一面窗，我能看的
就只有眼前嗎？
我還是習慣看看自己，
自己往自己的內心看……

（2017.10.09／17:48 在胡思公館店）

Beyond the One Window-pane

Through the window-pane, out of which, I look from inside,

In fact I should've looked inside from outside,

To put it more clearly, I should've

Looked into what's in my innermost in the heart

People outside come and go, what on earth is there anything to do with me?

Anyone else whom I should have thought about,

Not just seeing those coming and going passing by.

There are winds and rains, if the rain hits me on the face

Don't be mistaken I'm weeping tears. Feeling sad about the grieving past

What's more, as there are winds and rains to expect in the future

As a window pane, could I only see what's in myself just limited in front of our naked eyes?

Or just used to look at myself,

By looking at me in what's the innermost of my heart.......

小蝸牛和貓和我的一天

我將遠行，這件事
我早早就告訴了我家的貓，
我家的小蝸牛，牠躲在樟樹下
也聽到了！

今天清晨，我要出門時
我家的小蝸牛，牠起得比我
更早，
而且已經沿著我家的門牆
向上爬；現在我已經
到了機場，正準備登機
不知牠是否已上了我家陽台的女兒牆？
上了女兒牆之後，是否可以再往上爬
就能爬上雲端？

我在想，牠一向都走得很慢，很慢
我在想，我還是把牠和我家的貓，
一起帶在心上，
我上了飛機
我飛上了雲端，牠們也就可以一起
上了雲端
我們都了上雲端；

現在是傍晚，飛機剛降落在天河
我到了武漢，很快我們就可以進城
我家的貓和我家的小蝸牛，
我們都一起到了有一條長江
環繞著的武漢，
這就是我說的
小蝸牛和貓，和我的
一天。

（2017.10.13／10:20 漢陽西大街小學演講廳）

A Day in My Life with the Little Snail and the Kitten

I'm going on a long trip to a faraway place, this matter
Long ago I have told
The little house snail in my house, already hidden under the Taiwan Zhang camphor tree
It also overheard what I said!

Early this morning, when I was leaving home
The little snail, getting up far earlier than I did,
Having already crawled upward along the wall of my house; now I already have
Arrived at the airport, getting ready to board the plane
Wondering if it's already crawling into the protective lower-wall fence of my house balcony?
After reaching the top of the fence wall, whether it would go on climbing onward
Till it could climb over to reaching in the cloud?

I'm pondering, it has been walking very slowly, super slowly
I'm thinking, it'd be better to take it together with my kitten,
Both are in my heart,
I boarded the airplane
When I flew into the cloud, they both could go there together with me
In the cloud
We three all are in the cloud;

At present it's late in the afternoon at dusk, the airplane has just arrived at the river of the heaven
I arrived at Wu Han, shortly we would enter the city
My home kitten and the little snail,
We all got to the Wu Han City which is surrounded by the Yang-Tzu River,
This was what I had said
A day I spent with
The little snail and my kitten.

秋天，帶著桂花香進城

金桂，銀桂。我家有棵金桂，
種在家門口，我每天出門時
都愛在這棵樹下等車，
上車下車，也在這棵樹下

秋天桂花開，我家的桂花
也盛開；在金秋時節，
我每天出門都記得
要帶桂花香進城，
我回家時，也記得
要帶著桂花香走進家門

我的桂花香，夜裡
我不只留給自己，
白天，我會天天
帶去城裡……

（2017.10.30／08:27 在進城的捷運板南線上）

Going Downtown Carrying Autumn Sweet-scented Othmanthus Flowers

Orange Othmanthus, silver Othmanthus. In my house there's an orange or golden othmanthus,
Planted in front of the door of my home; everyday I'm waiting there for my bus to arrive,
I love standing under this tree.
Getting on and taking off the vehicle, also under this tree

In the fall, the othmanthus is fragrant in full bloom, so, as those in my home brightly blooming; in the
　season of orange othmanthus
Every day when going out of my house I'm surely inclined to remember
To bring othmanthus fragrant flowers with me to enter the town,
When going home, also remember
To carry some fragrant othmanthus flowers heading for my house e

My othmanthus flowers are so sweet scented, in the night
Not only do I leave it for myself,
In the daytime, I'll also bring them with me downtown. everyday......

蝶豆花茶的初戀

妳有海洋的藍，深邃
也有幸福的藍，清純
那個初秋的午後，
妳加上了
微酸的檸檬，妳也有了
不曾有過的紫色
初戀的憂傷！

（2017.11.09／23:25 研究苑）

First Love with Blue Butterfly Pea Flower Tea

You've got your sapphire ocean-like blue in color, so darkened deep

Also had the blue color hue of happiness, so fresh, clean and pure

In that afternoon of the early autumn,

You added

A slightly sourness of lemonade, then you've also got

The purple color that you haven't had before

As t the feeling of sadness and sorrow of your first love!

蝶豆花的藍

舒心之藍，藍它自己
可藍，可舒心，適合我
用它藍色調和我心中的塊壘，
畫它蔚藍天空和湛藍海洋，
任各類情緒的飛鳥魚蝦

……自在飛翔悠游……

（2017.11.10／14:01 研究苑）

The Blue Color of Butterfly Pea Flowers

The blue color that comforts, pacifies and stabilizes the heart, enabling itself

To be in blue hue, that can please my mind, and suit me for making me happy and contented.

Using its blue hue to moderate and mitigate the troubles and concerns in my mind,

To paint the azure sky and sapphire deep blue ocean,

Allowing all the flying birds fishes and shrimps with various feelings and moods,

Swimming and soaring freely at ease roaming leisurely........

旋轉的心眼

沒有花瓣，她還是花；
百香之果的心眼，
以花序之光芒，旋轉時空
旋轉戀人的思緒
讓他仰望，如仰望夢中
夜夜旋轉的星眼……

（2017.11.11／08:16 研究苑）

Cycling the Mind's Eye

With no petals, she's still called a flower;

The Mind's Eye of a passion fruit exuding from its heart eye,

The lighting beams of its flower inflorescence, revolving and rotating time and space around lovers, with
their thoughts and feelings

Letting him look up, like looking up in the dream at eyes of the stars

That are turning around whirling every night......

冬天，山裡的雨

冬天，山裡的雨
踢踏踢踏，常常不睡覺，
他們，男孩女孩都有
男男女女都愛在我屋頂上，
嬉戲，踢踢踏踏；
踢踢踏踏……

他們好像在跳舞。我在屋裡，
躺在床上，感覺他們的舞步
有時是整齊的，有時
就亂七八糟，
踢踏踢踏，踢踢踏踏
慢慢的變成滴滴答答，
滴答，滴答，
滴，答，滴，答……

剛開始時，我不是怎麼喜歡的
後來我也慢慢變成喜歡，
喜歡他們的演出；因為是
免費招待，感覺自己是很重要的
成為他們的貴賓，
十分榮耀！

（2017.11.16／07:17 研究苑）

In Winter, Seeing the Mountain Rains

In winter, rains fall in the mountain
It's raining pitter-patter and pit-a-pat, always making me not easy to fall asleep
They're all, both boys and girls
Men and women all love staying on my roof
Playing, tic- tic- tac- tac games;
Sounding Tic- tic -tac-tac, toc- toc……

They seem to be dancing while I'm staying in the house,
Lying on the bed, feeling their footsteps moving near, stamping and dancing around
Sometimes in a good organized order, sometimes
In a mess-up, and muddle at sixes and sevens.
Tic- tac tic- tac tic- tic tac- tac toc, like a clock ticking
Slowly and gradually changing into tic tic toc toc,
Tic toc, tic toc,
Tic, tac, tic, toc……

In the beginning, I didn't like it that much
Later I gradually and slowly came to like it,
Liking their performance; because it's
Free of charge, free admission or free pass, feeling I'm so important
To become their VIP guests,
Being very much honored indeed!

黑的，我心中有光

黑的，是的
我心中有光，
我不會害怕；
我的貓，牠是黑的
我喜歡說她，
不該說牠

她是我的，
我們常常在一起，
其實，我們一直在一起；
她在我心裡，
我在，她在
我們會永遠在一起。
黑的，是的
只是外面的黑，
我的心中有光，
我的心裡有她，她是我的
我的貓，她是黑的

（2017.11.29／19:04 捷運南港展覽館站）

In the Darkness There's Light in My Mind

It's black. That's right
In my mind, there's light,
I'm not afraid of it;
My kitten, it's black
I like talking about it,
But shouldn't criticize it

It's mine,
We always get together,
In fact, we've been getting together all the time;
It's being staying in my heart,
I am here, and it is present
We'll be together forever.
It's black, right
It's only black in its appearance,
In my mind, there's light,
In my mind there it or she, she is mine
My kitten; she's black

寒風中的野菊

未達萬苦，已至千辛
冷冷尖硬，刺骨
夜夜擁冰自囚；在石縫中，
年年夜夜，寒風親灼……

（2017.12.05／12:53 研究苑）

Wild Daisies Stand Erect in the Wintry Wind

Even not having suffered ten thousand pains, they've already undergone thousands of bitterness
Chilly, frigid cold with hardened points, with bone-piercing frigidity
Every night self-imprisoned in an icy cage, in the crevice of stones and rocks,
Year in year out, every night, personally in private with kisses planted on by wintry chilly wind……

冷，又想嶗山

冷，就該多想，想我嶗山的冬天
當會更冷
記憶中，除了光凸凸的山石
在石頭和石頭促膝頭碰頭的
空隙方寸裡，有翠綠的櫻桃樹之外
那四月春天還捨不得離開的季節，
櫻桃白色的小花兒是開給我欣賞的，
她們開開心心
看在我驚奇的眼睛裡，她們自己也是
驚喜好奇的凝視著我
光光的額頭眉下兩顆晶亮的眼珠，
想五六月那時節我早已離開，
但我的心和我的眼睛都會留下，即使
她們看我和我看她們的眼珠，
櫻桃早已成熟，應該就是朱紅的
更重要的是，你要是貪嘴
肯定也和我一樣，喜歡親親她們
就親親她們，親親她們……

（2017.12.17／19:31 研究苑）

Chilliness Reminds Me of Lao Shan Mountain Again

It feels chilly, so I should think hard more, about the winter spent in Lao Shan

It must've had been chillier

In my memory, except for the bleak, desolate and barren mountain rocks

Amongst the rock stones holding their head-to-head, knee-to-knee intimate téte-a-téte chat

In the narrow crevice,

There fit in other than the greening cherry trees,

In that spring season in April is still reluctant to part

The white little cherry flowers are blooming for me to appreciate

They're all so cheerful and delightful

Astonished, they themselves also felt so

Surprised to stare at me

The bald forehead under which two sparkling eyes,

Pondering on the season covering May and June when I've already left,

But I'll have my eyes and heart left behind with them, even if

They're looking at me and I'm gazing at theirs eyeball to eyeball,

The cherry fruits have already ripened reddened enough, in scarlet

Most ignorantly, if you're very much fond of eating so greedy,

You definitely would like to plant them a kiss like me

Then kiss them, kissing them, why not......

有，有，有沒有

有，什麼是有？
我口袋空空，
我腦袋滿滿；

有，別成為負擔
沒有，很輕鬆；

想，原來沒有的
就變有了！
想，原來有的
可以放下，
可以布施，
有，會變成更富有；

這些，有和沒有
都是自己想的。

（2017.12.22／08:40 去台中高鐵上，車過新竹）

Having, Owning, Have or Haven't

Have or Own, what's meant by "Have"?
My pockets are empty,
Yet, my brain is not; it's full;

To have or own, never make it a burden
Not to have or Haven't. It feels very light or burden-free, relaxing and at ease;

Think that, there's originally nothing that belongs to me
Now, it becomes something for me to own!
Think that, There's originally something to have
That can be let go of
That can be given away,
The, to have, can have more and become richer; for, to give is to take.

All these, "have's" and "have not's"
All are what's in your mind, depending on your own thinking.

閱讀大詩41　PG2109

 活著，在這一年
Staying Living and Lively, in This Year
——林煥彰中英對照詩集

作　　者	林煥彰（LIN, Fuan-chan）
譯　　者	黃敏裕（Min-Yu Morris HUANG）
校　　對	李美純
責任編輯	徐佑驊
圖文排版	周妤靜
封面設計	楊廣榕

出版策劃	釀出版
製作發行	秀威資訊科技股份有限公司
	114 台北市內湖區瑞光路76巷65號1樓
	電話：+886-2-2796-3638　傳真：+886-2-2796-1377
	服務信箱：service@showwe.com.tw
	http://www.showwe.com.tw
郵政劃撥	19563868　戶名：秀威資訊科技股份有限公司
展售門市	國家書店【松江門市】
	104 台北市中山區松江路209號1樓
	電話：+886-2-2518-0207　傳真：+886-2-2518-0778
網路訂購	秀威網路書店：https://store.showwe.tw
	國家網路書店：https://www.govbooks.com.tw
法律顧問	毛國樑　律師
總 經 銷	聯合發行股份有限公司
	231新北市新店區寶橋路235巷6弄6號4F
	電話：+886-2-2917-8022　傳真：+886-2-2915-6275

出版日期	2018年11月　BOD一版
定　　價	300元

國家圖書館出版品預行編目

活著,在這一年:林煥彰中英對照詩集 / 林煥彰
著;黃敏裕譯. -- 一版. -- 臺北市:釀出版,
2018.11
　　面;　公分. -- (閱讀大詩;41)
中英對照
BOD版
ISBN 978-986-445-297-2(平裝)

851.486　　　　　　　　　　107018687

讀 者 回 函 卡

感謝您購買本書，為提升服務品質，請填妥以下資料，將讀者回函卡直接寄回或傳真本公司，收到您的寶貴意見後，我們會收藏記錄及檢討，謝謝！如您需要了解本公司最新出版書目、購書優惠或企劃活動，歡迎您上網查詢或下載相關資料：http:// www.showwe.com.tw

您購買的書名：_____

出生日期：_____年_____月_____日

學歷：□高中 (含) 以下　　□大專　　□研究所 (含) 以上

職業：□製造業　□金融業　□資訊業　□軍警　□傳播業　□自由業
　　　□服務業　□公務員　□教職　□學生　□家管　□其它_____

購書地點：□網路書店　□實體書店　□書展　□郵購　□贈閱　□其他

您從何得知本書的消息？

　□網路書店　□實體書店　□網路搜尋　□電子報　□書訊　□雜誌

　□傳播媒體　□親友推薦　□網站推薦　□部落格　□其他_____

您對本書的評價：（請填代號　1.非常滿意　2.滿意　3.尚可　4.再改進）

　封面設計____　版面編排____　內容____　文／譯筆____　價格____

讀完書後您覺得：

　□很有收穫　□有收穫　□收穫不多　□沒收穫

對我們的建議：_____

_____

_____

_____

11466
台北市內湖區瑞光路 76 巷 65 號 1 樓

秀威資訊科技股份有限公司 　　收

BOD 數位出版事業部

....

（請沿線對折寄回，謝謝！）

姓　　名：_____　年齡：_____　性別：□女　□男

郵遞區號：□□□□□

地　　址：_____

聯絡電話：(日)_____　(夜)_____

E-mail：_____